Dog War

Dog War

Anthony C. Winkler

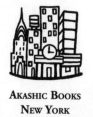

AKASHIC BOOKS
NEW YORK

Published by Akashic Books.
©2006, 2007 Anthony C. Winkler

Cover design by Daniel Sinker/Pirate Signal International
Author photograph on back cover by Collin E. Reid

First published in the United Kingdom by Macmillan Caribbean, an imprint of Macmillan Publishers Ltd. Akashic Books edition published under license from Macmillan Publishers Ltd.

ISBN-13: 978-1-933354-28-6
ISBN-10: 1-933354-28-3
Library of Congress Control Number: 2006936538

Printed in Canada
First printing

Akashic Books
PO Box 1456
New York, NY 10009
info@akashicbooks.com
www.akashicbooks.com

For the Levis: Michael, Suzanne, Amanda,
and Alison—doggone good neighbors

PART 1

Chapter 1

"Lawd, I beg you, don't drop a tin can 'pon me head today!"

So muttered Precious Higginson as she sat before her bedroom vanity and pinned her hair one breezy Friday morning in her Jamaican mountain home.

Whether the morning was windless or breezy, Precious began every day with the same muttered prayer, for she knew from bitter experience that Almighty God sometimes got vexed and threw tin cans from heaven above onto the heads of heedless sinners roaming the world below. Indeed, just such a thing had happened to her as a child and had made her forever fearful of heavenly braining.

Then a mere girl of eleven, she had been sitting under a tree with a neighborhood boy. They had played over and over with the few makeshift wooden toys, climbed four or five trees, scampered up and down the beach, and were quickly bored to tears. To perk up the hour, the boy suggested that they fish inside each other's pants to see what could be found there, and a squealing Precious was soon nastily groping down his drawers with all ten brazen fingers. The Almighty had witnessed the crime, and a few minutes later as Precious skipped merrily away from the scene of filthy fondling,

He caused a tin can to be blown out of the branches of a tamarind tree, bonk her sharply on the head, and knock her to the ground.

Mummy came running over, clucking with materialistic comment and explanation. What rude boy had thrown that can into the branches? How unlucky for her one daughter to be passing under the tree just as a breeze dislodged the tin can! Why must the world always be so nastied up by coincidence and gravity?

But Mummy did not know where Precious's fingers had just been digging this past hour or what forbidden part it had been fondling. Only Precious knew, and she had learned her lesson: Crotch fondling is not permitted without due authority of marriage paper. And if you don't obey His will in this and other matters, God will surely lick you down with a tin can.

"Don't drop tin can 'pon you head! Good God, woman, you goin' make de new maid hear you and walk off de job! God love a duck, somebody please tell me why de one wife I have in de world must start off every blessed morning with de same fool-fool argument."

So bellowed the gruff voice of Theophilus, who stepped out of the bathroom wearing only a frowzy pair of drawers through which the snout of his brown penis sniffed suspiciously at the morning breeze. Precious modestly averted her gaze.

Theophilus dressed with fuss and clatter, for that was his nature. He was a dark-brown man who had a craving for rule and regulation and always seemed provoked. His face had too much ridge and sharp bone to it. Nose battled mouth for dominance, chin feuded with cheekbones, a simian ridge erupted violently out of his forehead like a continental shelf, and all warring parts were sealed under a lava flow of contentiousness that curdled the corners of his mouth and gave him the deadpan look befitting his role as headmaster of a secondary school.

Precious stared at her reflection in the mirror, scanning anxiously for pore and wrinkle and marbled gray strands of hair on her head.

She was forty-seven years old and invitingly padded in the way Third World women used to be before austere American dietitians began to run amok over the globe. Barely scribbled on by middle-aged wear and tear, her face was buffed smooth of bump and wrinkle. She had a soothing, matronly face and always seemed happy and content, as if she might at any minute bubble into a smile or gurgle into a laugh. Her complexion was the rich brown of healthy topsoil, and so long as Theophilus didn't pester her, she was always as radiant as a godmother.

"Why pore must open up on me nose, eh?" she moaned at her reflection. "I wonder if I take too much condensed milk in me tea."

"Pore opening up on you nose because you start off every blessed day with de same fool-fool argument. Keep it up for another twenty-eight year and you goin' end up with a pothole on you nose much less pore."

"Mind you make de maid see you naked," Precious warned, as Theophilus backed out of the closet, carrying an armful of the day's clothes.

"Dat all right," snickered Theophilus. "De sight o' Brutus will sweet her and start her day off proper."

Then he deliberately and provocatively swaggered in full view of the open doorway while Precious stared with Bible-study attentiveness at a watermark on the bedroom ceiling and pretended she did not know who named Brutus or what on earth her husband was talking about.

She only knew that at forty-seven, even after twenty-eight years of marriage, she would dead before she addressed a penis by a Christian name.

Theophilus and Precious lived in an ancient wooden house perched like a jaunty schoolboy cap on the crest of a mountaintop. It was not the house in which they had reared their two children, both now grown and gone. Harold, their older child, was a dentist in Kingston with an island-wide practice and the father of two sons; Shirley, their second, was a Miami policewoman who had married a white American and borne two roughneck daughters.

The house in which these two had been raised was in Runaway Bay in a neighborhood where everything and everyone had been known, accepted, and familiar. For nearly twenty-eight years the Higginsons had lived there happily through the assorted childhood traumas of measles and incidental bruises; the woes of primary and secondary education; the post-adolescent muddling over career path; the tearful departure from the nest along with accompanying migration, marriage, and grandchildren. Precious would have been quite content to grow gray and stooped in that beloved old house, drop dead in her own backyard, and fly straight from Runaway Bay into well-earned heaven.

But then one morning Theophilus woke up craving a peak.

"A peak? What you mean?" Precious wondered, staring with perplexity at him over breakfast when he first raised the subject.

Theophilus sighed and brushed familiar neighborhood fly off his forehead.

Lately he had been restless, uneasy, not sleeping and snoring in his usual way, like a pregnant sow. Something was troubling his peace of mind, and now it was coming out.

"You know, Precious, I born and raise in mountain country. And every now and again when I look around me, I don't see a peak. Not a peak to be seen."

"For heaven's sake, Theophilus! What *are* you talking 'bout?"

"Mountain peak, Precious! What other kind of peak could I be talking about? Mountain peak!"

"Don't we have peak behind us?" Precious pointed at the shadowy drawing room wall behind which she knew, some miles away, loomed an unmistakable peak planted with tourist villas and apartments.

Theophilus scoffed.

"Dat is a hump, not a peak! Precious, listen to me, I have to speak me mind about dis! What I feel for is real mountain peak! You don't know how I have me heart set on a house where I can see peak morning, noon, and night! De children grow and gone. Tourists crawling all over Runaway Bay. We have one little fool-fool hump behind we. I need peak, Precious. I want peak. I crave peak."

Precious sighed. A twitch darted in the corner of her mouth like a pent-up guppy. "You want to move," she surmised.

Theophilus nodded eagerly. "To a place with peak, Precious! To de mountains!"

Precious stirred her tea and drew doubting breath. Finally she said, "Theophilus, I am not a woman to oppose her husband. You want a peak, you get a peak."

"God bless de day I marry you!" Theophilus exclaimed, leaning over and smacking a noisy kiss on her forehead.

Precious chuckled at his childish delight. "My goodness, Theophilus! You're very welcome!"

A few months later the Higginsons sold their old house in Runaway Bay and moved into the mountain home where Precious had just greeted sunrise with her usual morning prayer.

Chapter 2

The new house was in the district of Lime Hall over which mountain peak ran riot. Precious was one woman who preferred a soothing flatland to the unruliness of too much peak, and as she strolled in her garden before breakfast this morning, she could hardly bear to look at the surrounding skyline, it was so top-heavy and lumpy with mountain. Behind her was peak. To her left was a jumble of peaks, which dipped and slanted off into slopes curdled over with thicket and bush. Mist floated above the peaks, and the hillside of green thicket and dense bush was cobwebbed with damp slivers of ground fog. The only relief from the interminable clutter of peak was the distant scraped-clean ocean horizon.

Served by Maud, a woman with so little sense that they had secretly nicknamed her their fool-fool maid, Theophilus and Precious ate breakfast on the veranda. It was impossible to hire, train, and keep a sensible girl in a house so far atop a mountain and so deep in the bush, for she would not stay once she had trekked a few times up the winding marl driveway which even a hardened country cow could not climb without gasping for breath. Only someone truly fool-fool would work in an old wooden house rinded by gingerbread and planted in a puddle of grass on a mountaintop so desolate and barren that it was the ideal place for an escaped criminal to murder an innocent woman in her own bed.

Indeed, as a venue for slaughtering a helpless housewife, for tying her up on the bedpost and leisurely beating her brains out, this new house had no equal. No woman in the world could scream loud enough to bring rescue. Precious had proved this herself the very first day they moved in, by lying in her bed and pretending to be murdered by an escaped maniac from the lunatic asylum. She bawled that she was being butchered, raped, stoned, and clubbed, and after every anguished shriek for help, she had paused to listen hopefully for the scurrying footfalls of a savior. Not a one came. No matter how loud she bawled or about what fiendish and bloodthirsty torture ("Lawd God, he bite off me little toe!"), not even a peep rushed to her rescue.

When Theophilus came home after the first day that Precious had spent alone in the new house, he found her ready to move. She complained that she had taken vows to love, honor, and obey, but none required her to be slaughtered in a Godforsaken house just so a selfish husband could gaze upon mountain peak. They had a row about it, which meant that Theophilus tried to browbeat his wife into believing she had suddenly gone mad.

"Is it mad not to want to be murdered in your own house? You bring me up here so you can live among peak. Suppose a criminal come when you're at school. Suppose he bite off me little toe."

Theophilus glared at her with exasperation.

"Why would a criminal want to bite off you little toe?" he bellowed.

"Because dat's how criminal brain work! He might want to bite off me little toe, yes! He might want to do worse! What help would come? None, dat's what! None! He could take his own sweet time and gnaw off each toe even if he didn't have a tooth in his mouth."

"You just make me feel like I want to bite off you little toe meself! And maybe you two foot, too!"

"So now I must stay up here in this lonely house and be murdered just so dis man can see peak when him wake up in de morning!"

And so it went back and forth. Theophilus screamed and banged furniture and spoke longingly of how it would just sweet him to throw a woman off the side of the mountain. Precious rolled her eyes and said that she would gladly submit to being murdered by a heartless self-centered wretch of a husband, but please to carry her to a St. Ann's Bay lawyer so she could at least make her will and provide for the grandchildren. Night fluttered erratically around the house like a ratbat while the argument raged.

Finally they reached grudging agreement. Precious would get a job that would take her away from the despicable desolation in which she had been transplanted against her better judgment.

And for her protection Theophilus would buy two bad dogs.

Theophilus went out and bought two dogs. One was a big white dog; the other, a big red dog. When Theophilus had first brought the dogs home, neither he nor Precious could think of what to call them no matter how hard they rummaged through their stock of dog names. Precious suggested "Fido," which Theophilus said was damn French foolishness. Precious countered with "Poochie," which struck Theophilus as stupid (to prove his point he ran around the house bawling, "Here, Poochie! Come, Poochie!" and looked so ridiculous that even the fool-fool maid had to laugh). "Rover" was as American as rampaging gunman and just not suitable for a Jamaican dog. Precious suggested naming them after old-time Jamaican money, calling one "Thruppence" and the other "Sixpence," but Theophilus balked, saying that he was not prepared to name any dog of his a penny less than "Hundred Dollar." Precious said that such an exorbitant name for a dog would make people think they were secretly rich and draw gunmen.

After much back and forth over dog name, Theophilus declared that he wasn't going to get brain fever over it, and why didn't they just call the white dog "White Dog" and the red one "Red Dog." Precious agreed, remarking that since one dog was white and the other red their names had a sensible truthfulness.

From that day on the white dog was called "White Dog," and the red one "Red Dog."

Both White Dog and Red Dog proved to be hearty biters. White Dog loved to bite cow shank; Red Dog loved to bite human foot. White Dog would frequently go charging into the pasture whenever he spotted a cow that wanted a biting. Frequently the cow would disagree that it wanted a biting and would kick at him or try to buck him, but White Dog was usually too quick and would dart out of reach, circle, and get in a good nip on the shank of the beast, causing the terrified cow to stampede into the thicket, mooing.

Red Dog thought cow biting was infra dig and senseless teenaged fad. Human foot was what he loved to bite. Of course, there was little or no human foot in these remote parts, and what foot occasionally trampled the hillside was usually armed with a machete it was more than willing to use on a biting dog. Red Dog discovered this for himself the first time he tried to nip the heels of a drover in the pasture and got chopped for his trouble. He next tried to foot-bite the postman who had trudged up the hill to deliver a telegram and very nearly got his brains bashed out with a stick.

For a while after these misadventures Red Dog moped around the hilltop pasture looking forlornly on while White Dog frolicked about contentedly biting cow shank. Then one day, like a godsend, Red Dog spied the fool-fool maid trudging down the driveway and realized that all along right under his very snout was a human foot for biting. Red Dog catapulted off the cut-stone steps in an explosion of snarls and barks and hurtled at the foot of the maid, who was daydreaming about buying a new frock. The maid turned, glimpsed Red Dog thundering down on her, his fierce eye determinedly fixed on her foot, screamed, and flew up a tree. She sat clinging to a crook in the trunk, screaming bloody murder while Red Dog leapt and snapped at her dangling foot.

The maid remained stuck in the crook of the tree until Precious came home and threw stones at Red Dog and drove him off. As soon as she clambered down from the tree, the fool-fool maid spat out her notice and stalked off angrily. Precious chased after her and offered a dog-bite bonus of two hundred dollars if she would only change her mind and stay.

"I stick up inna tree for two hour because of dat dog and you want give me two hundred dollar?" the maid scowled. "Is two hundred dollar just fe climbing de tree?"

"Five-hundred-dollar bonus, den!" Precious countered. "Two fifty for de climbing, and two fifty for de near biting."

The maid scowled ever darker and scuffed at the gravel of the driveway with her toe.

"Is shoulda five hundred for climbing, five hundred for de time up dere, and a thousand for de near bite!"

"Lawd, Maud! How you so wicked, eh? I tell you what. Five hundred fe de climb, five hundred fe de time, and five hundred fe de near bite. A fifteen-hundred-dollar bonus."

Maud wrinkled her nose and grudgingly accepted.

That had happened months ago. Since then, Maud had collected two more fifteen-hundred-dollar bonuses because of Red Dog. One payment had been earned; Red Dog had really charged and treed her again. But the other episode had been a bogus vote. She needed a little extra money for her boyfriend, so she climbed the tree, straddled the crook with her bony rump, and hollered for Red Dog. When he ambled over to stare up at her with a puzzled expression, she threw him down a soup bone attached to a coarse string. Red Dog sniffed at the bone and settled under the tree to contentedly gnaw at its knobby end. At the sound of Precious's car approaching, Maud yanked the half-chewed bone out of his mouth, stuck it down the front of her dress, began blubbering for mercy and help, and so pocketed her bogus pay.

Even though Red Dog had proven himself useful for extra spending money, Maud still hated him with a passion. She saved all the choice morsels from the kitchen for White Dog, giving Red Dog nothing but gristle and scraps. One time she even stuck a bird pepper in his bowl of cornmeal. Red Dog took one greedy chomp on the pepper, exploded in a bewildered howl, and took off for the river.

"What happen to Red Dog?" Precious wondered, watching him tear down the hillside.

"Him don't like de cornmeal, mum."

Sometimes Maud would serve Red Dog bush mixtures in his food that would bind his bowels for at least a week. Then she would add a herb and give him a thorough washing out.

Precious had noticed Red Dog's peculiar bowel habits, and this morning she broached the subject with Theophilus while both dogs slumped on the cut-stone steps and covetously eyed their masters' breakfast.

"Dat dog don't doo-doo de whole week, you know dat, Theo?"

Theophilus looked stunned. "You follow de dog around all day to watch him doo-doo?"

"I don't follow de dog around, Theo. But I know how dat dog stay. You watch. One week he don't do anything at all. Not a lump. Not even a little dumpling."

"Lawd Jesus, woman, I eating me breakfast!"

"Sorry."

Maud had sauntered onto the porch during this exchange.

"Him goin' go this evening, mum," she promised inscrutably, collecting the dishes and trudging off toward the kitchen.

Precious shook her head in amazement.

"Theo, I swear dat girl is a prophet. She is always right. When she say Red Dog goin' doo-doo, is better dan money in de bank!"

Theophilus glared at his wife, a fork laden with green banana poised halfway to his mouth.

"I don't want to talk 'bout dog doo-doo when I eating me breakfast!" he thundered.

"Sorry," Precious said meekly.

Theophilus departed for school to preside over standing committees, blanch unruly bottoms, and teach Norman Invasion. As he clambered into his car, he took in a deep draft of the surrounding mountain scenery and joyfully bellowed with a magisterial sweep of his arms, "Now, dis is what man call peak! Dis is peak, Precious! See peak dere, and dere, and dere."

With Theophilus gone, Precious went into her bedroom, latched the door, and, before dressing for work, crawled under her bed to have a heart-to-heart chat with Jamaican Jesus.

She had talked to Jesus since she was a child, usually holding pious conversation with him in the open air as she walked down a quiet parochial road after church. But since her braining she just felt better about confessing sin when her head was shielded from blowing tin can by bedspring and mattress. So she took up talking to Jamaican Jesus while hiding under her bed.

In the beginning, she spoke to Jesus as if he were a foreigner to whom a Jamaican could not pray except in standard English with proper use of "who" and "whom." But then she attended a revival meeting one Sunday in which the evangelist proved that Jesus was indubitably a Jamaican for Jamaicans just as he was an American for Americans and Trinidadian for Trinidadians, for the reigning power of Jesus defied all earthly nationality and pettifogging borders. If a sinful sheep in Timbuktu called out to Jesus it was Jesus the Timbuktuan shepherd who appeared. How could it be otherwise? What would it be but errant colonialism for Englishman Jesus to appear unto Jamaican sheep?

It was a profoundly enlightening sermon to Precious and convinced her from then on to talk Jamaican patois to Jesus under her bed as if he were a street-corner higgler.

This morning Precious crawled under the bed and confessed to Jamaican Jesus that sometimes she was a little short-tempered with Theophilus, but he often drove her crazy with his constant yapping over peak without considering rape and murder of isolated wife. Jamaican Jesus said he was getting sick of all the gobbling about peak, too, and felt like giving the brute the tin can. Precious suggested that this Saturday night when Theophilus came to her for his weekly conjugal ride she would withhold pum-pum from sinful Brutus and teach him to hush up the infernal chatting about peak, but Jamaican Jesus said that for a wife to impose such a burden on a hard-working husband was slack and out of order.

Precious said yes, she supposed so, but added that not a day passed when she didn't feel put out with Theophilus for dropping her among wild mountain peak like an abandoned bird egg.

Whether all this was nothing but forehead gossiping with neckback or one sleepless neuron in the unlit occipital lobe whispering in tongues to another, it did not matter much to Precious. What mattered was that when she talked to Jamaican Jesus she always got a sensible answer and felt as comforted as a materialist with his martini.

A few minutes later Precious emerged from under the bed to work on achieving the flawless appearance that suited a Christian sister whose self-appointed mission was to serve as a human monument to piety and upright living for the backsliding riff-raff. She said goodbye to Maud and set out for the main road.

Because she did not have her own car and did not drive and Theophilus left too early for her liking, every day Precious had to tramp down a rutted marl driveway wearing her best work frock and meticulously manicured face because she lived in the Godforsaken bush, but never mind, she told herself grimly as she daintily avoided spiking cow pat with her high heels and pricked her way down to the asphalt road, wilderness was the price she paid to make her husband happy, the heartless wretch.

The thought of a happy Theophilus cheered her spirits so much that she began to warble a hymn as she walked down to the main road. It was not a vengeful hymn about slaughtering sinners and tossing them into burning pit—those were not hymns for a woman of her sunny disposition. Rather, it was a peaceful hymn about taking a boat trip across placid waters and reuniting with long lost friends on the far shore. Cows looked up at her as she walked past humming this hymn, because, as she noted to herself with quiet satisfaction, even an insensible bovine was drawn to melodically sung words of salvation.

She finally arrived at the main road, paused to apply one or two quick repairs to her grooming, before unfurling her umbrella and taking up roadside post to await a minibus.

This was another inconvenience that country dwellers had to suffer in silence—striking ridiculous poses on a desolate roadside while waiting for a rickety bus that followed no set route, came at no predictable time, and was frequently so crowded that a few unlucky passengers often had to ride with the top half of their trunks swaying giddily out the window.

After much baking in the hot sun while looking and feeling like a buffoon, she finally got a ride in an overstuffed country bus and arrived at her workplace, which was a hotel in Ocho Rios.

Being busy made the day fly by quickly, and soon Precious found herself waiting for Theophilus at her customary pickup spot just outside the hotel gate, through which a steady stream of waiters, gardeners, and maids poured out into the evening. He finally picked her up and they rode mainly in silence up to the remote country house.

It was Friday and traffic was heavy, the roads being clogged with lumbering trucks travelling between Kingston and Montego Bay. Theophilus drove too fast and several times she warned him about dangerous overtaking. He asked her if she wanted to drive, knowing fully well that she didn't know how.

It began to drizzle and several times the car skidded, but she said nothing. Her soul was ready. Let him drive as fast as he wants, she told herself fatalistically. She would only arrive in heaven early.

Chapter 3

Precious and Theophilus arrived home to find Maud standing in the doorway, waiting impatiently to collect her wages and go home. She had cooked dinner and left it sitting on the table, covered with a dishtowel against flies. Night was falling and the sinister dimness beginning to stain the bushlands and fields made Maud fretful and uneasy, for she was afraid of walking down the hill alone in the dark.

Precious paid Maud her wages and wished her a safe walk down to the main road. Maud sniffed and said she would be lucky if she made it to the bottom of the hill because it was already gloomier than usual for the time of the year and the road was dark and wicked. Gunman could hide behind any bush and she would see him only after she had suffered a fatal shot. Precious glanced expectantly at Theophilus, hoping that he would offer to drive the maid down to the bottom of the hill, but he was already at the table and facedown in his dinner.

"Well, do de best you can," Precious advised helplessly.

"If you find me dead body on de road, ma'am," Maud sniffled, "beg you tell me mother and see dat me get one Christian burial in Clarendon."

"De gravy gone to sleep," Theophilus growled, his mouth bulging full of food.

For Precious, Saturdays and Sundays on the mountaintop were days hollowed out with emptiness and boredom. The maid being off on weekends, there was no one to talk to, no passing pedestrians to ogle, no gossip to share and no rumor to monger. There was just nothing eyeball could see on these drab and wasted days but empty overgrown peak, and Precious could only putter about the house and garden and try her best to keep her mind occupied.

For the rest of the morning, she clopped around the house in floppy slippers making a stew for Theophilus who, as usual, had disappeared down to the corner bar to place a bet on the horse races, leaving her bouncing uselessly from one room to the next, straightening, dusting, sweeping here and there, fussing with doily and flower pot, while the seconds and minutes dripped interminably on her uncovered head. With the stew bubbling on the stove and cobweb routed out of every corner, she rattled down the porch steps and out into the garden to weed the flower beds and plant bulbs and seeds.

White Dog came loping over and sniffed her up and down as she knelt and hunched over the garden soil with her trowel. Red Dog soon ambled over and tried to add his own friendly lick.

"Yuk!" Precious snapped. "Dog tongue! Go 'way, dog! Come back when you have dry tongue."

Theophilus claimed that dog mouthwater was cleaner than a human's, but Precious still could not abide a nasty dog-tongue mopping, she was very sorry. She had seen with her own eyes dog nose skimming a hairbreadth above a cowpat. She had once seen White Dog jab his snout halfway up the crinkled pink batty of Red Dog and take a narcotic whiff that went straight to his head and made him giddy. That same nasty snout would brush against her skin over her dead body.

Precious was busily digging into the soil, kneeling on the edge of the flower bed and unwinding an endless worm from the roots of her gardenia bush, when suddenly she sensed a dog nose poised to spear deep into her own private batty. She turned quickly to see White Dog sniffing avidly at her nether parts with an excited quiver in his moist nostrils.

"Dog, you mad?" she asked, glaring at him over her shoulder.

White Dog guiltily backed up, ambled away, and slumped in the shade of a tree.

"Lawd, what a way you long!" Precious moaned, reeling the worm out of the soil.

Saturday night was Brutus's night to ride. In the early years of their marriage when Brutus was young and frisky, he rode as avidly and often as a bus passenger with an unlimited transfer. But with advancing age, Brutus had gradually settled for longer, less frequent rides, until his schedule had dwindled to this one compulsory Saturday-night outing. Rain or moonshine, starlight or fog, Brutus wanted a ride on a Saturday night.

Romping in the moonlight, White Dog and Red Dog could hear scuffling noises drifting from the darkened house and rustling the cool mountain vapors that floated over the pastures, and somewhere deep inside their dog brain they might have puzzled over why every Saturday night sounds of squeaking bedsprings, thudding bedposts, and human muttering came purling out the curtained window.

On this particular night, as the two dogs slumped on the grass and occasionally got up to pace and peer quizzically in the direction of the mysterious sounds guttering from the house, they both suddenly jumped at a piercing female shriek—a jubilant wail of joy, born-again vision, Irish sweepstake winnings—that rang from the darkened bedroom.

White Dog looked at Red Dog as if to ask if that was the mistress.

Red Dog stood up and looked back as if to scoff that Christian women like the mistress didn't make that kind of slack noise. Winding himself into tighter and tighter circles, Red Dog flopped wheezily on the grass.

A cool breeze wafted down the slopes, fanning the pastures with the sweet scents of wild mountain flowers.

Inside the dark bedroom, Theophilus was chuckling with manful triumph. "What dat noise you make, Precious? Brutus sweet you?"

There was an embarrassed silence, then a languid reply. "Theophilus, I believe you proper calling in life is pornography, you know dat?"

"Pornography, what! If Brutus sweet you, say dat Brutus sweet you! Nothing to be ashamed 'bout if Brutus sweet you."

A flutter of wifely resignation. "All right. Brutus sweet me. You happy now?" Bedspring cracked and creaked from the sounds of middle-aged bodies settling down for the night's sleep.

Theophilus chuckled. "Boy, Brutus! Middle age might reach you, but you can still do de job!"

And the whole domestic foofaraw was capped by a faint sigh of demure assent from Precious.

"Oh, yes!"

The Sabbath following was always devoted to hymning and praying off the effects of nasty carnality beastly Brutus schemed to provoke out of her every Saturday night, and that was exactly how Precious spent this Sunday. With a grumpy Theophilus in tow, she went to church determined to atone for her wanton squealing of yesterday.

Theophilus always looked sullen in church, and this Sunday he was no different. Church ached his back, aggravated his corn, gave him a buzzing in his ears, made his belly run. Not that he said or did anything disruptive or out of order during the ceremony. He just slumped in the pew looking woebegone and dejected.

The only time he would perk up was if a parishioner had dropped dead during the week and the minister had a few words of eulogy to say about the deceased. Theophilus would then instantly shed his gloominess and lean forward to listen. Afterwards, on the drive back up to their mountain house, he would moan about how only last week the faithful departed had been drawing breath and cussing bad word but now was dead and gone, carrying on quite as if no one in the parish was allowed to die without giving notice.

This Sunday they learned that an elderly gentleman who had lived in the parish for well over fifty years had suddenly died, and on the way back to their mountain home Theophilus as usual was carrying on as if the deceased had not well outlived his promised three score and ten.

"Safe and happy at last," Precious opined solemnly.

Theophilus gritted his teeth and the gear of the car as he steered up the steep and narrow road.

"Precious! De man is not safe and happy. De man is dead and gone."

"My faith tells me dat he is safe and happy," Precious replied, cool as river rockstone.

"I suppose when I dead and gone you goin' talk 'bout how I safe and happy, too!"

"Theo, you not goin' dead and gone for many, many years. And knowing your disposition, even when you safe and happy, you probably goin' carry on miserable and cantankerous just to be contrary. But I not worried. My God know how to handle you."

They drove the remainder of the way up the hill cobwebbed in the stolid silence of the long-married.

That very next day Theophilus, recklessly overtaking a van around a corner, collided headlong with a semi truck and instantly became safe and happy.

Or dead and gone.

Chapter 4

Sudden death brings out the best in neighbors. It makes them boil soup and bake pies and brings them filing to the casket to mutter consolations and peer grimly at the deceased. Even acquaintances who had not particularly liked Theophilus in life, finding him too this or that for their taste, in his death were quite willing to drive up the hill and lament his passing, hanging head as if their best friend had been struck down.

Shirley, the Higginsons' one and only daughter who was now a Miami police, came to Jamaica for her father's funeral, bringing her gun but leaving behind her husband and children. She explained that she did not agree with children attending funerals, for she had had to undergo just such a trauma at the age of ten and it had given her a lifelong dose of the heebie jeebies. She would never permit her own flesh and blood to experience a similar shock.

The dentist son, Harold, attended the viewing and funeral with his wife, Mildred, and his two children, both of whom gambolled in the front yard, skipping and throwing stones and drawing occasional scolding from mournful adults. One of the children, the boy, was romping with White Dog when Red Dog snuck up and tried to nip him on the foot. But the boy was already schooled in the sneakiness of dog and as soon as he realized that Red Dog was out for a nip, he kicked him briskly on the snout. Red Dog yipped that he was not a football and

22

scurried for the underbrush, tail between his legs, with the boy scampering gleefully after him, trying to punt him over the gully mouth.

The adults congregated solemnly in the wooden house on the hilltop, drinking fruit punch and rum and viewing Theophilus, who was laid out in a draped black coffin on the dining room table, braced against the burdensome weight. One woman remarked how well Theophilus looked and expressed the wish that she, too, would look as good at her own viewing. Another opined that the dead headmaster didn't look a day over thirty-five. A third decried the waste of burying a man in such a good suit when so much ragamuffin abounded in Jamaica, but another declared that she intended not only to be buried in her best frock, but also in her pearl necklace, for she knew perfectly well that if she didn't carry the necklace to her grave her husband would hand it over to another woman, and she damn well didn't buy a necklace to hang from any other neck but her own.

Milling with swarms of black-garbed mourners, the gingerbreaded house looked like a rookery of fretful crows. Breeze blew, and low clouds scudded over the mountain ridge and frothed up a gray drizzle that edged the proceedings with a shudder of gloom.

Then the funeral procession of cars undulated down the rough mountain road like some disjointed beetle humping its sluggish path to a dreary burrow.

Precious was heartbroken. Caring for the throng of mourners, having to endure sympathetic scrutiny for days on end, was all that saved her from utter collapse under the weight of her grief. She could not cope with the idea that Theophilus was gone, really gone forever, and the one time the awful truth struck her was when she was thankfully shielded from prying eyes by the bathroom walls. She crumpled over the sink and wept inconsolably. Someone tapped softly on the door, and Precious muted her wild sobbing, dabbed her eyes with a towel, and regained her composure.

Just before Theophilus was hoisted on the shoulders of friends and neighbors and borne away in the hearse, Precious stole a quiet moment to whisper her final goodbye.

She was staring at the buffed body splayed out in the stylized pose of death and reeking of the undertaker's powdered fondling when, on an impulse, she reached down and stroked for a last time the white gloved hands entwined in a mound of doughy fingers atop the unmoving chest and whispered, "Goodbye, Brutus."

"Who's Brutus?" she heard someone hiss in her neckback. She glanced behind and saw that her daughter had overheard.

"No one," Precious said stonily, turning back to the coffin.

"But who's Brutus? That's not Daddy's name! Tell me?"

"It's private."

"Private? I want to know who's Brutus and why you calling me daddy Brutus when his name was Theophilus!"

Precious backed away from the table and stared helplessly as the pallbearers hoisted the coffin and shuffled with it toward the hearse parked on the front lawn.

"You goin' tell me 'bout Brutus?" Precious felt the daughter's breath pelting the crease of her neck.

"No," she shot back over her shoulder.

The mourners slow-marched out of the house and across the creaking wooden porch.

"That's why I turn police, you know dat!" the daughter whispered angrily. "Because you and Daddy always kept things from me. Always!"

Overcome by the senseless futility, the dizzying absurdity of the moment, Precious stumbled vainly after the coffin. Hands reached out and brushed at her with sympathy. Behind her sulked the fiery daughter, scowling with resentment and insistently hissing, "Why can't you tell me *who* name Brutus?"

The first three or four nights after the burial were oppressive but bearable. Family and friends gathered around and filled the threatening emptiness of the mountain house with the patter and prattle of ordinary life. The daughter slept beside Precious. The son occupied the room next door and made the wooden house quiver with the healthy footfalls of a preoccupied man. Friends came and went, bringing with them a train of petty affairs, gossip, and neighborhood stories; and the unrelenting silence that stalks every widow was kept at bay for a week.

But then the friends drifted away, one by one, and the visitors dropping by with a cake or a pot of stew peas came less and less often. The son disappeared for longer and longer stretches, and finally one morning he packed up and returned to his own household in Kingston.

Shirley lingered in the mountain house for another week. She slept every night with her policewoman's gun under the pillow, snoring and gnashing her teeth something fearful. One night she sat upright slowly like an uncoiling spring, extended her finger, took sinister aim, and cocked her thumb as if it were the hammer of a revolver. The dream gun went off noiselessly in the shadowy room, and each time it recoiled and jerked in her hand as if it had actually spat deadly bullets.

"Me God!" Precious breathed fearfully as Shirley crumpled beside her in bed.

The daughter replied with a nasty snore and rumbled over on her belly.

Awake early the next morning to a dawn still creamy with curdled mists and swirls of nighttime fog, they sat in the drawing room drinking breakfast tea.

"Mummy, what you goin' do?" Shirley asked earnestly. "You can't stay here by youself. Look at dis place!"

She waved her hands at the slabs of dour mountains and scowling ridges jutting through the mists.

"You shoot a man in me bed last night." Precious tried her best not to sound as if she were complaining. "Me nerves not used to dat."

"Dat's what Henry always tell me," Shirley grinned.

"You mean you sleep-shoot all de time?"

The daughter shrugged. "According to him, one of dese nights is him I goin' shoot."

There was a delicate pause. "You not getting along with you husband?"

"We get along all right, Mummy. Him is just too . . . too . . . if you know what I mean."

"Just too-too. Well, dat's not so bad. At least him don't carouse at night and beat you."

"Beat me? You want me kill his rass! I tell you de God truth, Mummy, I only keep him because of de children. Dey just love deir too-too daddy. If it wasn't for dem, I'd pitch him right out de front door."

Precious put her foot down and delivered maternal homily. "You too Americanized! A woman must respect her husband."

"Respect his rass! He can kiss my batty!"

"Mercy!"

Shirley leaned over the small tea table in the drawing room around which they were huddled in bathrobes against the morning dampness and stared hard at Precious.

"Why you don't go live wid Harold in Kingston, Mummy? Lock up dis Godforsaken house and go where you have company around you. Do it, Mummy!"

Precious looked dubious. "Two woman under one roof," she muttered lamely.

"Den come to Miami and live wid me! I would love to have you under my roof!"

"But would your husband like dat arrangement?"

"Him either like it or lump it! No too-too man goin' tell me whether or not I can have my modder in *my* house. I goin' apply for you paper when I go back."

Precious felt so helpless and befuddled that she could only gaze idly around the room picking out familiar objects and pieces of furniture, her eyes roaming over nook and cranny and corner as she vainly tried to think of what to say, what to do. In her momentary confusion she could not even think of where to put her hands or rest her elbows, and all her upper limbs suddenly struck her as having been maliciously glued on in the wrong places overnight. She counted the fingers on her right hand, found them to be five, and then counted the ones on her left hand, and was briefly startled that they were the same number. Everywhere she looked she saw the signs and treasures of a living, breathing Theophilus—his favorite chair, table, couch, cushion—but no Theophilus. She imagined that she could even smell Theophilus in the room and had a feverish notion that if she could only glance about her quickly enough, she would glimpse him hurrying down the shadowy hallway or leaning against the kitchen doorjamb.

But the room was full only of wisps and memories. It was hideously empty of Theophilus.

As if she had read her mother's despair, Shirley reached over consolingly and patted her hand. "Never mind, Mummy.

And as long as I draw breath, you will always have a roof over you head."

Then Shirley was gone back to Miami, leaving behind a fearsome silence that made Precious feel like she constantly needed to scurry to the bathroom. Maud stayed two nights after that on the mountain to keep her mistress company, but on the third night she abandoned Precious to the bush. There was just too much croaking lizard up here for her taste, Maud grumbled. She never knew that night could be so long and dreary, that wooden house could crack and pop so much. It sounded like gunshot in her weary head. She had not slept a wink in two nights and would rather dead now and get it over with than suffer through another night of croaking lizard and popping wooden house, she was very sorry.

Precious stood on the veranda and watched the maid trudge determinedly down the hill that third evening. White Dog came nuzzling up, begging a pat on the head. Red Dog watched the maid's foot wistfully as it pistoned out of reach down the marl road.

"I see you early in de morning!" Precious yelled as the maid rounded the corner.

"If life spare, mum," drifted the dour reply from around a hump in the hillside.

There is city night and there is country night. City night is leaky with light from houses and apartments and noises from the street; but even in the thickest slab of darkness, there is always at least one insomniac fearfully counting his daytime sins by a bedside lamp.

But country night is a lidded pot into which light and sound do not drip. When there is no moon to softly yellow the land, when there is only the gravel of stars glowing in the immense darkness, a widow cowering alone in her house sees country night as abandonment by God, as the end of all hope and dreaming. And so the night seemed to Precious the first time when she was truly alone, when she turned off the lights in the hilltop house and took to her empty bed.

She went to bed at 9:00 and woke up at 9:15, feeling as if she had just crawled out of the bottomless crack of sleep into which she had fallen. Night fluttered blue and silken over the pastures and the hilltop house as she lay still and suffered demented visions about a rapist.

In her fretful imagination, she saw the rapist get off the bus at the bottom of the hill and clamber up the rutted marl road in the darkness, pausing once to sharpen his butcher knife.

She crawled under her bed to fearfully consult Jamaican Jesus about what she should do, but He had nothing to say and she gathered from the silence that He had gotten fed up with her 'fraidy-'fraidy nature and taken a minibus into town. She grudgingly muttered, "Thy Will Be Done," and crawled back out from under the bed nursing grievance and feeling like an old cow Jesus had chained to a tree and left in the bush. Of course, she would show Him once her throat was cut and her body fluids spilled over the polished floorboards. He would hurry apologetically to her side to escort her into paradise and rue the day He had left her defenseless among desolate peak. But if that's the way Jesus wanted it, bring on de rapist and madman! And with this wordless invitation, she peeled back her bronze neck-bone to the starlight, spitefully longing for two necks, nay, three, to be cut twice and thrice and prove once and for all who among the flock was truly a fearless, unwavering, and obedient sheep.

When the mad rapist did not immediately oblige, Precious thought better of it, turned on every light in her bedroom, and put on six extra panties. Then she turned off the lights and slunk back in bed and waited, hearing the brute panting and blowing and complaining grouchily to himself that the hill was long and steep.

With the elastic band tourniquet of seven panties choking off the blood supply to her liver and kidneys, to say nothing of her belly, she lay still but could hardly breathe much less sleep.

At 10 o'clock she grasped that she was a ridiculous fool and a brainless idiot, lurched angrily out of bed, and defiantly shed the extra panties.

She stood by the dark window and gulped several lungfuls of sweet nighttime mountain air through the burglar bars before crawling back to bed and tumbling once more into a troubled sleep.

She awoke an hour later, stared groggily at the face of the bedtime clock and glimpsed that it was now 11:00, that the night was not even half over, and began to suffer another deranged nightmare, this one about her murderer.

Lowly bus was not good enough for the murdering beast of her fevered imagination. Nothing but a cab would do, which he rode to the bottom of the hill, quibbling over the fare and leaving no tip as you would expect from a heartless wretch. Trudging up the hill, he paused to cut a hefty tree limb, good for bashing a defenseless woman's brains out. She saw him pulverize a coarse rockstone on the roadway with one swing of the club before being satisfied that it would well crack a skull and starting again up the hill in the starlight.

While he stomped brazenly in the darkness toward her house, Precious jumped up and rashly turned on the light, muttering to herself that if she had to be murdered in her own bed among wilderness and peak, she would at least be murdered in a decent dress. After all, she reminded herself deliriously as she scuttled about the bright room looking for just the right outfit, a woman got to be murdered only once in her life and certainly had no excuse for not being properly groomed for the occasion. When the police found her body, they would know right away that she was a respectable victim and not some common Butu. She would wear such a fine dress that the Homicide sergeant would just feel to take off his hat and bow his head with respect upon finding her black-and-blue corpse.

Trussed up in her best white frock like she was at Easter Sunday service, she settled back in bed and patiently awaited the killer while staring sightlessly at the dark ceiling and dreaming of the gallows and the last long walk the murdering wretch would have to take down a sooty hallway to the waiting hangman. She consoled herself just before dozing off fitfully that at least her torso would be well dressed for her death picture in the *Gleaner* and, although she would really prefer if the nasty newspapers did not show her to the whole world with her head bashed in, she supposed that there was no gainsaying modern photojournalism.

She fell into another mire of sleep, jumped awake at 12 o'clock to sleepily wonder what on earth she was doing in bed wearing her best dress. She got out of the frock and back into her nightgown.

Darkness held the wooden house in a death grip. The night stalked around her bedroom like a thief, tapped fingers against her window, popped and cracked ankle bones in her ear. It made her start; it made her heart lurch and race, her eyelids twitch and jump. She saw many horrible visions and suffered fretful nightmares of creatures and beasts seen only in dreams. Jamaican Jesus was nowhere around.

She sprang out of bed, padded to the closet, scooped out every shoe box and knick-knack that had accumulated on the bottom shelf, packed three pillows inside and clambered in, pulling the closet door firmly shut behind her. She was encapsulated in an airless and unimaginable blackness where not even the most cunning and bloodthirsty murderer would think to look for her. It was the same closet where Theophilus kept his shotgun propped up in a corner, and her big toe brushed against the cold wooden gunstock. Here she settled, cocooned in a womb of blackness like an enormous grub, and finally fell asleep.

But just before she dozed off, she muttered angrily, "Theophilus, you see how you leave me! You and you peak!"

The next day when Harold stopped by the house and perfunctorily renewed his offer for her to come and live with him in Kingston, she did not utter a peep about "two woman under one roof," she did not hesitate over her job; she just knew that as long as she drew breath, she would never willingly spend another night alone in that house.

She packed up a few belongings and rode into Kingston with her son.

Chapter 5

Mildred, the woman Harold called "wife" and under whose roof Precious now lived, was queen of a Kingston household in which cockroach dared not venture, fly met sudden death, and even the fleeting glitter of the joyful firefly was extinguished with aerosol spray. She served no custard at her table, harbored no pudding, tolerated no tambrin balls, no bullah cake. She was a woman with an unbridled appetite for discipline and scrimping.

In this household maid and helper came and went like summer rain. Those who stayed took fiendish delight in female ruff and rule, suffered mouth crimp, and sported the bony batty of deep-water fish. Antiseptic, enema, and washrag were inflicted routinely on the children. Man was forced to walk the straight-and-narrow path and encouraged to wallow in guilt over bad habit. Belly did not grow luxuriant and demon rum was never drunk except after funerals.

Into this tundra of temperance, frugality, and prudence came to live Precious, creating the turmoil of two women under one roof.

Two women under one roof: One loves pudding, the other loves bone. One has shaved off her batty with gruesome American aerobic exercise and diet, smiles only with a squint, and always chews with her mouth closed. The other is carefree and roly-poly, boasts the succulent and good-natured rump of a heifer, takes sweetened condensed milk in her tea, and is ever ready to forgive backsliding. One talks fast with words that hiss out between her teeth, the other chats slow with mouth open wide and well-fed tongue wriggling sinuously over moist lips. One makes music by drumming fingernails on tabletop, the other hums and warbles as she blusters through the house spreading sunshine and cool breeze. One the wife, the other the mother. Between them, Harold the husband, who wants only to live in peace and quiet and pull teeth. But war has broken out in his household between the woman who bore him in her belly and the one who rides him.

Household war number one.

Mildred does not like the way Precious slouches. She has read in a book about the insidious nature of bad posture, which can encourage criminal tendency, to say nothing of wreaking injury to backbone. She says the mother-in-law is always leaning against door frame, sagging against wall, slouching against couch and cushion, and the children are beginning to grow lean and crooked from bad example. Precious is hurt that she is thought to lean and sag when in her heart she feels sure that she stands straighter than church pillar and post. Mildred explains that spinal injuries are permanent and disabling; that American doctors say bad posture caused the fall of Rome; that Japanese children, who are the brainiest anywhere, stand straight as chopsticks, which just went to show you. Not because she lived in Jamaica did Mildred not keep up with American pediatric thinking. It was nothing personal, but please do not always tilt like faulty watchtower and hold up the doorway when the children are around.

Precious withdrew to her room, leaving Mildred reigning over the drawing room in which the first blow had just been struck.

Mother-in-law blood was spilled on the floor. Eyeball could not see it, but it seeped there from a grievous belly wound.

That night Mildred explained the argument to Harold, pointing out the viciousness of slouching, saying that it was nothing personal and she hoped Precious didn't take criticism to heart, but she was a woman who just had to rule her own roost.

Then to sweet him up, to show Harold who was who and make sure he took her side in the quarrel, she gave his bamboo a friendly little rub.

Since it was the first unbegged-for rub his bamboo had got in a long while, Harold quite forgot himself, grabbed his bony wife, and eagerly French-kissed her.

She pulled back and yukked. "Lawd Jesus, Harold!" she said with disgust, running to the sink to rinse out his nasty and unasked-for man mouthwater flooding her back teeth.

Remembering that she had had good reason to rub the bamboo, she sidled back into the bedroom to mollify him.

"You know I can't stand a tongue-suck unless I'm prepared," she said with a sniff.

Then she went off to ride her stationary exercise bicycle, leaving her husband, who was himself unridden for well over a fortnight, standing there stewing in backed-up bamboo juice.

He sulked in the drawing room and tried to read a dental journal. Precious was nowhere to be seen. The children were doing homework in their bedrooms. A single moth bobbed and darted neurotically around the blazing hallway light.

Harold rapped softly on his mother's door. "Mummy, you don't have to lock up all night, you know," he said plaintively.

"I not lock up," the faint reply drifted from behind the closed door.

"Come out and talk to me, nuh, Mummy?"

"I have a headache, Harold," came the halfhearted lie.

He went back to his journal.

The next day as he was jerking out a molar, a poor fat countrywoman wriggled in the chair, grabbed onto its armrests for dear life, and bawled bloody murder, "Sweet Jesus, Missah Dentist! Who trouble you, sah?"

Household war number two was fought over contraband pudding.

Precious cooked up a creamy pudding for the children, who went mad with joy over this unaccustomed treat. Mildred came home and went on a rampage. She did not want her children being fed nasty pudding, which had neither grain nor fiber and was bound to cause acne and running stomach. Why must she tolerate overrule of standing orders under her own roof? She had a good mind to fire the maid.

"But me don't do nothin', mum!" yelped the maid.

"You know I don't allow pudding in my house! How many times you hear me say dat pudding is worse dan cockroach poison? And you sit dere and let Mrs. Higginson, who don't know better, brew pudding in my kitchen?"

"Me never know she goin' feed it to de children, mum!"

Precious tiptoed away and hid in her room while domestic tirade raged in the kitchen. There was a soft knock on the door, and her grandson timidly peeped around the dusky doorway.

He sat on the bed beside Precious in the dimness and put his small arms consolingly around her neck.

"Grandma, when I grow up," the boy vowed fiercely, "I having pudding with every meal from breakfast to supper. Some meals, I goin' eat nothing but pudding!"

In the boy's eyes Precious saw smoldering the stubborn defiance she had grown to love in her own Theophilus. She chuckled and gave him an impulsive hug.

That night Mildred explained to a harassed Harold that rule could not abide under the same roof with overrule. One must stay and one must leave, for either rule prevailed or overrule ran amok and spread rebellion. Harold did not understand, but he did his best to listen magisterially while his wife related a skein of intricate and aggrieved detail about the quarrel over pudding.

"You same one say dat sweets cause cavity!" Mildred fumed piously.

"True," Harold nodded, solemn as a judge. "Sweets do cause cavities."

"Sugar is as bad as rat poison!"

Harold balked at this, and snidely remarked that sugar was as bad as rat poison only to American yuppies.

Sensing that he was turning contrary on her, Mildred wriggled up beside him on the couch and began to fondle the bamboo.

There was nothing erotic or loving to her touch, for she was a hardheaded wife who over the years had evolved economical action for repulsing Harold's annoying sexual begging. Moreover, she was one woman who only touched up the conjugal bamboo when she wanted something. But this was war to the death. On the one side was old Mummy who commanded the respect that came from nostalgic memory of cradle rocking and batty wiping; on the other side was lawful wife entrusted with custody and control over the household bamboo, with plenary power and authority to quell its periodic uprisings.

Mildred pursed her lips grimly. She would show once and for all that the hand that held the bamboo was ten times mightier than the one that had once wiped the batty. It would be pen against sword all over again.

Harold lay back on the couch panting weakly while his wife sternly shucked out his love-starved, neglected bamboo from a thicket of drawers flap, pants fly, and crooked zipper.

When she was done with him, Harold wore a pasty look of stupefaction and pleasure on his face that said he was primed for twirling around her finger.

She twirled him as she stuffed the dead bamboo limply back into its gabardine dungeon.

"You know I like you mummy, Harold. It's just dat she must not overrule me."

Sprawled on the couch, Harold could only give a piggish oink of happiness. "If you would only do dat to me once a week," he whimpered.

"You see how you stay! De more you get, de more you want! Instead of being grateful for what you get, you want more!"

"I don't want more," he lied weakly.

"All I ask is to be able to rule me own roost. Is dat too much?"

"Mildred, Daddy just dead. Mummy all alone. She need us."

"Did I tell him to dead? Don't everybody must dead when deir time come? Don't even I must dead one day?"

"Mildred, please try to understand."

"I do understand. Is my fault that you daddy dead. I must pay for his reckless driving."

Harold squirmed and gave up. He muttered that he would have a heart-to-heart talk with Mummy.

Precious endured three months of this loveless treatment, feeling like a barefoot urchin in Mildred's kingdom. For the sake of peace she even made an effort to sweet-up Queen Mildred, to show that she was ready and willing to bow down before the lawful ruler and mistress of the household, but even this harmless bowing and scraping backfired.

Mildred had cooked up a batch of stringy dried-out muffins and, biting into one, Precious had behaved as if she were eating heavenly manna.

"Dey're dry," Mildred growled sourly, curling lip at her own muffin.

"No," insisted Precious politely, "dey well moist."

"How can anybody in deir right mind call dis muffin moist? Taste this muffin, Agnes," Mildred commanded the maid. "Tell me dat dat muffin not dry."

Agnes nibbled on a muffin rind and winced. "It well dry, ma'am," she announced distastefully, washing down the pebbly crumbs with a tumbler of water.

Backed into a corner by her own inept attempt to kowtow, Precious shoved half the muffin into her mouth, chomped down hard on it, and felt it crack against her teeth like rinsed gravel. "Dis is a moist muffin," she persisted cheerfully.

"If you think it so moist, why you don't eat another one," Mildred challenged, a malevolent fire ablaze in her eye.

"Gladly," Precious murmured, picking up another and attempting to bite heartily into it while the maid watched and shuddered.

"See!" Precious lied, swallowing another slab of muffin masonry. "This is a moist muffin. Very tasty."

Grimly trying to bore a hole in the concrete kitchen floor with an impatient tap of her high heel, Mildred scowled as she watched Precious chew. "So eat another one den, if you think dem so tasty!" she flung.

"Lawd Jesus, Miss Mildred," Agnes protested, "you goin' bind de poor woman bowels with you dry-up muffin."

"*Me* bind her bowels?" Mildred snapped shrilly. "Don't I say de muffins are dry? Don't she insist dey're moist? How I

binding anybody's bowels? You see me holding open her mouth
and stuffing dry muffin down it?"

Precious tried to scoff but found that she could barely open
her mouth, for her teeth were temporarily cemented together
by muffin plaster of Paris and her tongue wriggled vainly in a
body-cast of gummy muffin batter.

"Mmmmooiissst," she lied determinedly.

She staggered out of the kitchen with as much dignity as she
could muster, closed the bedroom door behind her, and
sat down on her bed, certain that her days of carefree,
unmedicated doo-dooing were gone forever.

For two weeks after that Precious lived on magnesia and
epsom salts as muffin bone took its own sweet time about
scraping through her large intestines. She drank copious
quantities of water, went on long walks, even lay flat on her
back and exercised, all in a desperate effort to unbind her
system. Agnes seemed to understand her torments and
sympathize, for one morning as Precious stood by the sink
drinking her second tumbler of water, the watchful maid shook
her head sadly and muttered, "When Miss Mildred bind a
belly, dat belly well bind."

Precious stared at her with indignant astonishment.

"What you talking about, eh?" she asked, refusing to
acknowledge that a domestic possessed insider knowledge
about her bowels. "I'm fine! I just went!"

As she sallied off to her room she added acidly over her
shoulder, "That is, if it's any of your business!"

There would be other skirmishes later, rear-guard action,
ambush, blitzkrieg raid. The issues would vary—wasting
expensive electricity knowing fully well that money didn't grow
on tree; quibbling with maid over established household

procedure; countermanding garden-boy standing watering instructions for rosebushes—but it all boiled down to two woman under one roof, wife against mother.

Precious could not cope with the incessant clamor. She got so that she was afraid to make a move in the house for fear of sparking a row. She walked on tiptoe around the mistress of the house. She tried her best to make friendly small talk with the maid but always ended up feeling like a meddling colonial power.

One night she wept quietly in her bedroom while gazing at a wallet-sized picture of Theophilus dressed in his Sunday finery, his head tilted to one side as he glared stonily at the birdie with his usual tutorial grimness. Stifling and breezeless, the lowland stagnation typical of a Kingston night resounded with a cacophony of yapping neighborhood dogs, the occasional wail of a siren, the malcontent rumble of a foraging truck. Her airless windows were laced with ugly wrought-iron burglar bars filigreed into whorls and smothered under a bank of crinkled nylon curtains.

"What I goin' do, Theophilus?" Precious whispered bleakly to the photograph. "I not welcome here."

Just then the phone rang and the maid bawled for Miss Precious to come take a long distance call.

Precious leapt off the bed, deliriously wondering how Theophilus had managed to get through from heaven so quickly, and found her daughter on the other end of the line.

"Mummy," Shirley said in an exultant voice over the transoceanic static, "I pull string and get you a visa. You coming to Miami to live with me!"

Chapter 6

Four harrowing and busy weeks followed Shirley's call, during which Precious endured buffet and setback with a cheery countenance and unshakeable faith. Her dignity suffered numerous nicks and scratches from the American Consulate, whose staff, it is widely known, is globally trained to behave scornfully toward prospective immigrants, especially those whose grovelling is regarded as halfhearted.

But once it became clear that the interloping former batty-wiper was to be sent packing to Miami and that there was soon to be only one woman under her roof, Mildred displayed a more hospitable frame of mind and actually started holding friendly chats with Precious at the breakfast and dinner table. She even confided that ever since the birth of their son, Harold had contracted a sickly obsession with tooth extraction that sometimes drove her up the wall.

Precious remarked innocently that she didn't know Harold had any obsessions. Why did she think Harold had founded twelve clinics over the countryside? Mildred asked pointedly. It was for the sole purpose of providing him with countrywoman tooth to pull, which he accumulated in a shoe box like he was some kind of bizarre hobbyist. Precious said she didn't know that Harold collected teeth, so Mildred went rummaging through Harold's den and returned with a Bata shoe box that rattled when she walked. She pried off the lid to reveal hundreds of rotted teeth that stunk like old fish-bait.

"My heavens!" Precious gasped, peering into the box in which teeth of every shape, size, and state of decomposition were strewn in an untidy mound.

"Can you imagine? Dis is your son's hobby!" Mildred shook her head sadly in a manner that implied faulty mothering.

"I never tell Harold to pull anybody teeth," Precious mumbled in her own defense.

So things were better at the Kingston household and the time flew past quickly. There were a hundred little chores to tend to and a clutch of petty details to contend with. Precious made periodic trips with Harold up to the mountain house to pay Maud, brush dog head when White Dog and Red Dog came scampering to greet her, and generally check on her property. But she could not make up her mind about what to do with Theophilus's dream house. When she strolled around the grounds and fondly recalled Theophilus's love for mountain peak, she simply couldn't bring herself to sell it. Plus she did not think there was another person mad enough in the entire parish to want to live in such isolation.

One day during an infrequent visit to the house, Precious idly asked Maud, "What I goin' do with dis house, eh?"

Maud squinted and pursed her lips with deep thought. "If fire start up here, God willing," she suggested with a crafty glint in her eye, "no amount of fire brigade goin' reach dis hill before de house burn completely down."

"I goin' to write dat remark down in a book," Precious snapped.

Maud's eyes widened with alarm. "What book?"

"I don't know. I only know dat dat is de very kind of remark dat need to write down in a book. I goin' to buy an exercise book and write it down. What's de date today?"

"Miss Precious!" Maud squealed. "Don't write me down in no book, mum! All me say is—"

"Don't say it again," Precious threatened, "or I will have to write it down in two book."

"Everything up to God, mum," said Maud, hoping to sweet up her employer with religious argument.

"Exactly so," seconded Precious.

And, as far as Precious was concerned, that was the end of a particularly vulgar line of thought. She would not burn down Theophilus's dream house, and no amount of maid scheming would turn her into a firebug.

"You love to pull teeth, eh, Harold?" Precious asked her son on her last night under his roof.

She had said her goodbyes to the children, cemented an uneasy peace with Mildred, and now late into the evening with the rest of the household abed and migration staring her in the face, she was spending a final few fidgety minutes in the drawing room with her son.

He peered at her sharply. "Who tell you dat? You been talking to Mildred?"

Precious squirmed, not wanting any part in a domestic spat between her son and his wife. "I hear you have a shoe box full of teeth."

Harold sniffed with pleasure. "And every one of them I pull out myself!" he declared proudly. "With these two hands."

"Well," Precious mumbled, feeling stupid, "at least you have plenty teeth to play with in you old age."

Harold yawned, for the hour was late and he had spent the evening involved in the bustle of packing up Precious for shipment to America. Plus there had been a meal on this last night, and his belly was crammed full of egg foo yong and chop suey.

"Mummy, I sorry you and Mildred didn't get along. But she is a woman with her own ways, you know."

Precious shrugged. "Two woman can't live under one roof." She added gloomily, "Forty-seven years old and I'm going abroad for the first time in my life. Watch the plane crash tomorrow and kill me."

Harold seemed not to have heard. He suddenly leaned forward in the chair with a strange light shining in his eyes.

"One of these days, Mummy," he whispered after darting a furtive glance at the dark hallway over his shoulder, "I going pull one of Mildred's teeth. You wait and see."

"Almighty in heaven, Harold!" Precious yelped. "A husband not supposed to be sitting down in him drawing room planning to pull out his own wife teeth! You're out of order!"

Harold shrank from this unexpected blast, looking hurt and puzzled. "So now you taking her side against me!"

"You men are impossible! Is not enough dat you always want pum-pum, now you want teeth, too! My motherly advice to you, Harold, is to leave Mildred's mouth alone! A married woman mouth is her last refuge!"

Precious stood up to signify final opinion, stern motherly judgment, and the end of discussion. Harold remained glued to his chair, scowling and shuffling his feet like a chastised boy who thought his punishment overly harsh.

She withdrew down the dark hallway to her bedroom to lie in bed staring fretfully at a ceiling and listening to the metronomic fluting of a whistling frog, who piped the same monotonous and unwavering tones over and over again as if he had been made in Japan.

Chapter 7

You get to Miami from Jamaica by crowding aboard a brushed-metal pipe outfitted with clumsy appendages and pretending that it is right-minded and Christian to sit with strangers thirty-thousand feet up in the breeze, as if beneath your feet is the comforting solidity of God's good ground. Or so it struck Precious, who on the roaring and quivering take-off of her flight muttered a prayer aloud that drew an inquisitive stare from the businessman sitting next to her.

"I am ready to go," Precious announced when she realized that the man was staring curiously at her.

"Go where?" he asked suspiciously, the pipe tilted at a dizzying angle and thundering into the sky.

"Up there." Precious pointed at the sloped ceiling of the climbing aircraft. "If He calls, I am ready to join my husband."

The man grasped her meaning and didn't particularly like it. "Go where you want to," he grumbled sourly. "I'm going to Miami. I not going anywhere else."

"He leads," replied Precious stoutly, "and I but follow. Where He leads, I go."

Just then the aircraft shuddered and trembled as if it had hit a bad stretch of gravel road, and Precious gave a little squeak of terror, closed her eyes, and muttered a fervent prayer.

The man bolted up, gathered his briefcase, and shuffled up the aisle as far away from Precious as he could get.

"Thy Will Be Done," said Precious aloud as the aircraft flew into a cloud that pummelled its riveted body with invisible fists.

"Amen, sister! Amen!" bawled an old Jamaican woman sitting behind her. The aircraft gave a sickly wobble. "If dis be de time, I am ready!" the old woman crooned.

"So am I!" Precious flung piously over her shoulder. "Ready as ready can be!"

"Show me to de land, oh Lord!" bellowed the old woman with a tinge of hysteria in her voice.

A stewardess hurried over to stand beside them. "Would you please not talk so loud!" she ordered briskly. "We're in turbulence and you're frightening the other passengers."

"If dey be not ready, dey should well be frightened!" croaked the old woman.

"Amen!" seconded Precious.

"Hush you mouth!" hissed a young mother sitting across the aisle with her small child. "You frightening me pickney!"

"Lamb need not be afraid," rasped the old woman. "It is craven old sheep dat should tremble."

"Ladies, please!" pleaded the stewardess as the plane shuddered from a solid body-thump.

"Yes, sir!" squealed the old woman in a quaky voice. "We lick a good pothole dat time."

"But no fear in we heart! For we know we destination," reminded Precious, turning to mutter between the seats.

The plane rocked and dipped and yawed like a carnival ride. "Now is perfect time for a hymn!" the old woman croaked.

Then she began to sing "In the Sweet By and By," joined in by a shaky Precious whose usually melodious voice wavered and cracked with every lurch and shudder of the metal pipe in which she was sealed and fastened high up in the breeze.

When the plane finally landed with a jerk and taxied to a stop, the old woman breathed a loud sigh of relief and proclaimed, "Thanks be to God! We reach safe!"

But by then Precious had regained her sense of earthbound composure and was too embarrassed by her pushy airborne evangelism to offer any reply but the backslider's halfhearted "Amen."

The entire planeload of people shuffled through the tubular corridors that unwound to the mêlée of Customs and Immigration Clearance, Precious hangdog and blushing at the scowls and dirty looks darted at her by fellow passengers.

She arrived at Shirley's house to a splatter of wet kisses from her two grandchildren, who danced and skipped gleefully at her coming to live with them, and a warm but reserved greeting from Henry, the too-too son-in-law, who was a doughy-faced white man with red hair and a freckled nose. The children paraded her through her new bedroom, prancing and jumping beside her with uncontrolled excitement and delight as though she were a new puppy. They showed her the bathroom, the closet, the kitchen, the cellar, squealing over every revelation. They took her to the backyard tree house, which both of them scornfully explained they were too old to enjoy anymore.

Cheryl-Lee, the younger daughter, confided in her about that nasty Timothy Pigeon who lived down the street and whom she intended to punch out next time he snickered at her in the school hallway. Henrietta, the older one, interrupted with superior criticism: As far as she was concerned, punching out a geek like Timothy Pigeon was not worth the trouble. Certainly, it was not worth detention. Precious lectured in a stern grandmotherly voice that Jamaican girl children did not punch out boys, but then she quickly bit her tongue when she remembered that she had once knocked out a boy with one thump outside the tuck shop after he had squeezed her batty without permission. Cheryl-Lee wanted to know what a girl in Jamaica would do if a Timothy Pigeon was always snickering at her, and Precious lied and said that she would ignore him. How could you ignore a geek? Cheryl-Lee asked insistently. Precious did not know what a geek was, and was about to ask when Henrietta suggested that instead of punching out Timothy Pigeon, Cheryl-Lee should drop a lizard down his pants. Cheryl-Lee thought that was a wonderful idea and asked her sister to help her catch a lizard for dropping down Timothy Pigeon's pants, and the two children gambolled off down the street promising to return as soon as they had found the right-sized lizard.

Groggy with a hangover and befuddled at the newness all around her, Precious wandered back into the house where she found that Shirley had strapped on a gun under her armpit and was ready to leave for work. She kissed Precious goodbye and drove away after telling Henry not to cook any dinner for her since she would not be home until about 3:00 in the morning. Then Precious was left alone with Henry, wondering if she should warn him that his daughters were out looking for a lizard for Timothy Pigeon's pants.

She decided that she shouldn't interfere. Her brain was still thirty thousand feet in the breeze. She was in a place which struck her as strange as the moon and made her feel like a gate-crasher at a wedding.

She excused herself, went into her bedroom, closed the door, and crawled under the bed to catch her breath and take stock.

Precious took stock. Except for the distant burble of the television in the drawing room, the household was quiet. From under the bed, America reminded her very much of Jamaica, the cobwebs under the bed being uncannily alike in either country. The stale mustiness of the mattress and the comforting dimness of the airless crawlspace between bedspring and floor were quite what she was accustomed to find under a Jamaican bed. If she didn't know better, she would even think that she was under her own bed in Runaway Bay after a row with Theophilus.

It was still hard for her to believe that Theophilus was dead, but if he was dead under the bed, the one place where Precious always stared unflinchingly at the truth, then she could be quite sure that he would be just as dead in the open air. Her house in the Jamaica mountains was locked up and periodically tended by Maud, whom she had employed to tramp up the hill three times a week to dust and look after the dogs. She was still in a muddle about the house, but even her decision to let matters rest as they were for the time being didn't seem so confusing under the bed.

At her age migration was certainly only a temporary measure. She did not really think that she would be living in America for the rest of her life, but she had had to get away from Harold's house with the perpetual fussing and turmoil. Now that she was under a bed in America, she could plainly see that Mildred was wrong to snoop on Harold's tooth-box and begrudge a hard-working man his hobby. But Harold was also wrong in his scheming to pull Mildred's teeth. Yet Precious also had a sneaky feeling that Harold wanted to pull Mildred's teeth because Mildred was being a Dog in the Manger with the pum-pum. Long experience had taught Precious that when a wife starved her husband of pum-pum, the husband was likely to plot to pull out her teeth.

Her reverie was interrupted by a creak of her bedroom door. She glanced over the cobwebbed floor and glimpsed a small brown face peeping inquisitively at her from the edge of the bedspring. The face melted in the bedside gloaming and, after a flurry of pattering feet, a child's excited shriek of discovery rang through the house, "Grandma's under the bed! Grandma's under the bed!"

Precious hastened to wriggle out from under the bed just as there was a rap on her door and the pasty face of Henry swivelled around the jamb.

"Precious," he asked solicitously, "are you feeling all right?"

"I feel fine," Precious declared with dignity.

"Cheryl-Lee said you were under the bed."

Precious brushed herself off, opened her mouth to make an indignant denial, but resolved that migration and green card would not turn her into a liar.

"Dat is where I do my best thinking," she sniffed.

Henry, looking scientifically interested in this new thinking technique, cocked his head and approached.

"I better make sure I dust and vacuum under your bed, if that's the case. You might be spending a good deal of your time under there." He bent down on his knee and peeked under the bed. "I'll get the vacuum right now," he announced.

"You don't have to vacuum . . ." Precious started to protest, but it was too late.

A few minutes later he returned and vacuumed thoroughly while Precious sat on the edge of the bed, twiddling her thumbs and feeling like a fool. He scurried down the hall and returned with a throw-rug, which he placed on the floor, saying that it would be easier for her to slide under the bed if she first lay with her back on the rug. He demonstrated by sliding smoothly under the bed with his back flat on the throw-rug.

"It's rather snug under here," he said from beneath the bed, his voice taking on a slight metallic bedframe echo.

He slid back out, stood, and carefully arranged the rug with his foot. "I must try thinking under a bed sometimes," he chirped. "Maybe it'll help me clear my head."

Precious tried to make some noncommittal reply but managed only a disgruntled growl.

Cheryl-Lee stood in the doorway solemnly bearing witness to the whole proceedings. "Daddy," she asked quietly, "can I think under Grandma's bed, too?"

"I don't know," said Henry, looking nonplussed at Precious. "I think you better ask Grandma."

"Grandma?" the child asked piteously.

Precious sighed, thinking that she had never before in her life met a man that she would rather thump down on the spot more than her American son-in-law.

"I suppose so," she grumped.

The child giggled, lay on her back on the rug, and shot under the bed. "It's dark under here!" she squealed.

She scooted back out and propped up her elbow on the rug. "Grandma, will you come under here with me?"

So Precious reluctantly had to get down on the floor and slide under the bed with the grandchild. Soon Henrietta popped in and demanded to think under the bed with Grandmother, and before long Precious found herself pinned under the bed between two squirming children while Henry bent down and shouted encouragement and thinking technique at them.

"Did you find a lizard for Timothy Pigeon?" Precious asked in a whisper, propped snugly on each side by the wriggling bookends of her granddaughters.

Henrietta giggled. "Yes! You wanna see it, Grandma?"

"But don't tell Daddy," Cheryl-Lee warned. "Or he'll tell us not to do it."

"Don't worry," Precious whispered back. "Knowing your father, he might want to bathe de lizard to get it ready for Timothy Pigeon's pants."

Both children cackled gleefully at this idea, shaking so hard on the tiled floor that they vibrated Precious between them.

"Everybody still cozy under there?" Henry sang out in the daybreak treble of the capon.

Chapter 8

Every home is a honeycomb of intersecting routines, private ceremonies, and personal habits. And so was the one in which Precious now lived and to which she tried to adapt. The children had their fixed schedules of school and play; Shirley had her bizarre police work that gave her the nocturnal habits of an owl, departing in the evenings for night patrol and returning early in the morning when the children were first stirring; Henry had his beauty shop where he gave perms and managed a staff of five beauticians, requiring him to leave shortly after the children caught the school bus and just as Shirley was settling down for her day's sleep.

For the first week Precious was caught up in adapting to this hustle and bustle of intersecting domesticity without getting in anyone's way, but after only a few days she had such a good grasp of who should be awake when, who should be rushing out of the door, who should be settling down for a day's or night's sleep, that she could contribute to the smooth running of the household in little helpful ways by settling down this one, fixing a snack for that one, or playing the cuckoo clock for any who overslept. Having served her domestic apprenticeship under the most cantankerous man to ever step foot across threshold, Precious was grimly of the opinion that no man or woman born was her match when it came to mastering household quirks and complicated timetables.

That Henry was a beautician struck Precious as suspiciously odd if not downright unmanly, but she was careful to keep a straight face and offer no unwanted criticism. She just knew in her heart that she would never sit down and chat about women's hairstyles or perms or hair straightening with Henry no matter how hard he begged. If he wanted to discuss the criminal mind, slaughter in Africa, or the guttersnipe tactics of English football hooligans, she was more than willing to reply to the extent of her ability to hold intelligent conversation on these male topics. But if he should broach the subject of perms or dyes or hairstyles to her, she intended to yawn politely and remind him of his manhood.

During her first few days in America not an hour passed when Precious did not stumble upon a stupefying sight that made her just feel to stop and stare. America struck her as vast, strange, bizarre, and its exotic newness would have overwhelmed her senses and made her giddy had she not determined ahead of time to sternly repel geography. Of course, she knew that her foot now walked the shores of a far-flung continent, but she would still not allow herself to be bullied by the atlas. She remembered that Theophilus had told her that when he was in America, for one whole day all he could think about was, "Rass, dis place big, you know!" and that even as he stood at a urinal he had found himself silently and obsessively muttering, "Rass, dis place big, you know!" over and over again. But that was Theophilus. He was willing to kowtow to geography. Precious, on the other hand, knew who she was and what she was and was determined that no amount of continental land mass or foreign spectacle would reduce her to spatial muttering in the toilet.

Still, the first few days stunned her with such an unexpected array of sights that for nearly a week all she could do was gape and gawk. If she was not careful, migration was going to turn her from a decent Christian woman into a Peeping Tom, she told herself sternly in the evenings during contemplative moments of retreat under the bedspring, and while she did her best to refrain from staring, she could not help herself when she encountered outlandish scenes she had seen before only in Cinemascope movies.

It was not so much the foreignness of the place, for as a Third Worlder of moderate means Precious had been amply exposed to glimpses of America in television, movies, and magazines and knew what to expect. But what stunned her on her first drive through America was that the whole place appeared spanking new and shiny. Compared to Jamaica, which seemed steeped in a perpetual mildew and grubbiness, America shone as if it had just been polished. But the curious thing was that it was a shine and a sheen visible only to new immigrant eyes, for when Precious repeatedly mentioned how America looked gleaming and shiny to her, Shirley said gruffly that the whole stinking city was getting nasty and shabby, that Precious felt as she did only because she couldn't yet see American grime. There was Jamaican grime and there was American grime, and your eyes had to get used to American grime before they could see it. For an example, she pointed to a white man slumped against a bus bench and said that he was an American beggar, and when Precious looked at the man and saw that he was not only white but that he wore shoes and a presentable pants and shirt, she scoffed and said that such a man certainly wouldn't be a beggar in Jamaica, to which Shirley replied, "Exactly! What dey call poor here is a joke to us. Is de same way with grime. Our grime is not deir grime and deir grime is not our grime, even though an ignorant person might think dat grime is always grime," and Precious felt so stupid and put in her place that she stopped passing comment about America and contented herself with merely gawking.

Precious made one last brave attempt to defend her maligned Jamaican senses and score at least one point by sarcastically remarking to Shirley that at least murder was still murder in Jamaica or America and the two countries had that much in common. But Shirley again scoffed and said that murder in Jamaica was one body with a machete chop or perhaps one measly bullet hole, but that murder in America was at least two bullet-riddled bodies along with a gunman suicide. That was real murder, not your fool-fool garden party that know-nothing Jamaicans called murder.

Precious sat glumly in the front seat after that and held her peace, for the discussion was beginning to give her a complex. Shirley drove slowly through one neighborhood after another, past shopping malls and stores and parks, and tried to point out all the sights and places of interest, but because of her complex, Precious could hardly concentrate enough to listen. Finally she blurted out, "I not going let you give me a complex. I say de place look shiny and new. And it look shiny and new. And dat is dat."

"Mummy," Shirley chided, "this is not Jamaica."

"I am aware of dat!" Precious grumbled. "But you can't do everything better dan us! You can't have you own special grime dat only you can see! And you can't murder better dan we murder! Out of order!"

"Mummy, I'm just saying dat we do things big here. We don't murder one like Jamaicans do. We bag ten and fifteen on de spot. Sometimes we bag twenty-five, thirty."

"Stop you boasting! And stop running down you homeland! You born and raise in Jamaica, too!" Precious said shrilly.

And she steadfastly refused to listen to any more of her stuck-up daughter's patriotic ranting and raving.

The hardest thing for Precious to get used to was the constant spectacle of whiteness all around her, the unending procession of white face after white face frothing down the streets and through the malls in a perpetual tide of foam and spume.

The first time, for instance, when Precious came across a white man digging a hole in the sidewalk of a street, she could not help but stare, for she had never before in her life seen a white man even carry a pickaxe in broad daylight, much less raise one to dig a hole. Of course, one knew from books and the cinema that white men did such things abroad, but schoolbook knowledge was simply not the same as seeing with one's very own eyes.

She had been strolling with Shirley and Henry and the two grandchildren toward their car in the parking lot of a shopping mall when she spotted the white man digging the hole in the sidewalk pavement. Beside him leaned a big-belly black man who peered captiously down the hole and bellowed criticism and commentary over the digging. Precious stopped and stared, her mouth agape, at this scene from a movie.

"What you looking at, Mummy?" Shirley asked, edging closer and licking an ice cream cone.

"A white man digging a hole in de sidewalk," Precious mumbled.

"Damn lazy brute dem," Shirley groused. "Dey work for de government. If it take a normal man an hour to dig de hole, it take dem five."

"But digging a hole!" Precious mumbled, confused. "I never know white man could dig hole."

"Who say dey can dig hole? They're damn lazy! You want to watch?"

Precious muttered that she did not, for she felt vaguely queasy at the thought of sticking her nose into another's business, but Shirley had already seized her firmly by the elbow and was half dragging and pushing her across the striped parking lot toward the edge of the road where the men were working, all the while whispering to the children that Grandma had never before seen a white man dig a hole and wanted to see such a wonder up close for herself.

"Is that true, Grandma?" Cheryl-Lee asked in a whisper, excitement shining in her eyes. "You've never seen a white man dig a hole?"

Precious tried to mumble something in defense of this embarrassing shortcoming in her upbringing, while doing her best to shake off the official police death-grip with which Shirley steered her across the parking lot.

"Sometimes our garbage man is a white man, Grandma!" Henrietta blurted, skipping merrily at her side.

They were within earshot range of the digging men now, and Precious could even hear the big-bellied black man complaining about the depth of hole.

"It got to be deeper, I tell ya!" he was twanging to the white man, who was so deep down the hole that only his blood-gorged neck blazed above the ragged rim. "I know the line's down there someplace! You just gotta keep digging!"

The white man hoisted the pickaxe and drove the blade into the earth with a porcine grunt, while the black man slouched with his hands resting heavily against his knees and peered attentively into the hole.

"This is fun!" Cheryl-Lee announced. "Watching a white man dig a hole!"

"How come we never did this before, Mommy?" Henrietta asked peevishly in a tone that implied maternal neglect.

"Lawd Jesus, Shirley!" Precious muttered, tugging at her daughter's sleeve. "Dey goin' see we watching dem. Come, make we go back!"

Shirley kissed her teeth in an expression of contempt.

"I am a taxpayer," she growled. "I have the right to watch any man dig any hole so long as is my taxes paying for it. I am sitting right here and watching my taxes at work."

She sat down stubbornly on the curb, licked her ice cream cone, and watched the white man dig. The children plopped down in an arc of silence and studiously peered. Henry leaned against the trunk of a tree and looked amused.

Before long they could hear the white man groaning that the sun was too hot and the work too hard, and he and the black man withdrew under the shade of a nearby tree and lolled against its trunk, chatting and swatting idly at the swarms of hovering gnats and flies.

"See what I tell you!" Shirley said triumphantly. "And you say white man can dig a hole! Dig an inch and him take a half hour break! Damn lazy brutes." She lumbered to her feet and started across the parking lot toward the car.

Though the men had seemed oblivious to their presence, Precious thought some polite explanation of the family's gawking necessary. With Cheryl-Lee hanging onto her hand, she strolled over to the panting white man whose face was broiled a florid and ugly red by the exertion and the hot sun and said, "That's a very nice hole you were digging."

The man looked at her quizzically, turned to his black companion, and asked, "What'd she say?"

"Grandma says she like the way you dug that hole," Cheryl-Lee explained primly. "This is my Jamaican grandma," she added.

The men whispered and stared as the family retreated

toward the car parked in a distant corner of the enormous striped lot.

"I felt some explanation was necessary," explained Precious as Shirley drove out of the parking lot. "So we wouldn't seem uncouth."

"Lawd God, Mummy," Shirley muttered. "You don't understand dis country, you know!"

"I just wanted to compliment him on de nice hole!" said Precious stoutly. "Hi! What's wrong with dat? Henry, what's wrong with dat?"

"Nothing!" agreed Henry brightly. "That man has probably dug a hundred holes without a single compliment from the public. I think it's very thoughtful of you."

"You would," Shirley carped.

"I didn't think there was anything wrong with saying something nice about the man's hole," Precious mumbled defensively.

But Henry couldn't leave matters resting on that shaky note. He had to press ahead one obnoxious step further.

"Let's play a game!" he said brightly, turning to the children in the backseat. "Grandma isn't used to seeing white workers. From now on until we reach home, let's find examples of white working men for Grandma."

"Lawd Jesus!" protested Precious.

But it was too late. All the way home the children intermittently exploded into piercing squeals of triumphant discovery, crying out, "White man trimming a hedge!"

"White woman mowing the lawn!"

"White man walking a dog!"

"That doesn't count! That's not work! Does that count, Daddy?"

"White man painting a fence! Hah! That counts!"

Before long the two daughters were fighting over the passing pool of working white men, as each pirated examples from the other's hard-won stock.

"That was my white man in the tree! Wasn't that my white man in the tree, Daddy?"

"I saw the white man painting the fence first! Didn't I, Daddy? That's my white man!"

"I have five white men and you only have two! Nah nah nah naaah na!"

"Dad! Tell Henrietta to stop! She's provoking me!"

"The white man in the tree belongs to Henrietta. The one walking the dog doesn't count. But the one painting the house is Cheryl-Lee's," adjudicated Henry with a Solomonic air.

Shirley drove home with a sullen scowl.

That evening as Precious lay on her bed thinking about the day's contretemps, she heard the door creak open and saw Cheryl-Lee framed in the doorway. "Grandma," the girl asked timidly, "can I come in?"

"Of course, darling," Precious welcomed, reaching out for her.

The child hurried over, snuggled against her grandmother, then squirmed away. "Can we go under the bed and talk, Grandma?"

"We don't have to go under de bed. We can talk right here."

"But I like it under the bed, Grandma!"

Precious sighed. "All right," she said heavily.

Soon they were scrunched under the bed. Precious heard footsteps briskly approach her door and Shirley call out, "Mummy! I gone to work. See you in de morning."

"Goodbye!" Precious bellowed back.

She heard Shirley ask in a puzzled tone through the closed door, "Why Mummy sound like she so far away?" and Henry answer nonchalantly, "Oh, she's probably under the bed. She goes there a lot."

"Henry, are you driving my mother under a bed?"

"I didn't do anything but fix up under the bed for her!" Henry squealed.

Shirley's footsteps beat a brisk tattoo to the front door and a few minutes later Precious heard her car drive away.

"Grandma," Cheryl-Lee asked petulantly in the under-bed dimness, "didn't I see the white man painting the fence first?"

Chapter 9

There are men who are brutes, drunkards, and lazy good-for-nothings, but the too-too man is the only kind a woman constantly has an urge to wash out with an enema. A woman likes a man with gristle in him, one she can sink her teeth into and chew on happily for years as a lifetime cud. Theophilus had been just such a tough-skinned wretch: cantankerous, miserable, headstrong, set in his ways; always trying to shish kebab pum-pum with everlasting pushy, forward, impertinent, rude, and out of order bamboo; always bawling about his dinner, complaining about his clothes, ranting and raving at maid and mistress. If ever a man had gone straight to heaven it was that gluttonous, never-satisfy, big-belly soul, and Precious just lamented the day the wretch had to go and collide with a truck around a corner, stranding her in America with a too-too man for company.

It was morning. Precious and Henry were at breakfast, with Shirley asleep and the children gone to school.

Henry was fussing about the kitchen, provoking Precious to inwardly fulminate about him in this vein as he fried her an egg she did not want, had not asked for, and was perfectly capable of frying for herself if she had felt for an egg, which she did not, although the brute still insisted on frying one. It was a perfectly fried egg, with not a trace of grease or singed lacy edges, and

Henry had just carefully slid it onto her plate like a Frenchman dishing out a serving of bullfrog foot.

She stared hard at him and swallowed her peevishness.

"Precious? You want any orange juice?"

"No, thank you."

"Does my juice have too much pulp?"

"I just don't feel for any orange juice."

"I don't mind squeezing a fresh batch, you know!"

"Lawd Jesus, hanging on de cross!" Precious whispered.

The too-too man was right and correct in everything he did or said in the irritating way of the catechism. You could not say that he was *too this* or *too that* because if you did you would seem an ungrateful wretch. You could not find the proper words to express your grievance about such a man without appearing small-minded and petty. So you held your peace and kept quiet, and this very suppression of righteous irritation made you feel strongly to kick him down and reach for your enema pan.

Henry was such a too-too man.

Precious baked banana bread. She had taken a job at a temporary agency and on her first day off she spent the whole morning baking, and when the children came home they snacked happily on the warm banana bread as they chittered about their schoolday adventures.

Henry came home that evening and counterattacked with his own banana bread, claiming that he had been meaning to make it from last week but kept forgetting, and since Precious made her bread and the children had so eagerly eaten it, he would cook his own too while the pans were still warm.

So Precious was forced into waging banana bread war with a man.

And the wretch had the gall to win.

His banana bread was plainly better than hers as she could tell from the very first nibble. Then he suggested that hers wanted more vanilla and sugar.

Precious stared at him with disbelieving eyes, wondering how much she was expected to endure for a green card.

"How many perms you set today?" Precious flung spitefully at him as she retired to her room, where she crawled under the bed to nurse grievance.

A few minutes later came a tap on her door.

"Hullo?" cried Precious, sulking under mattress batty.

"Are you thinking, Precious?" Henry asked through the closed door.

"Yes, I am."

"May I come in?"

"Why? You want an enema?" she mumbled.

"What did you say, Precious?"

"I said, one minute, please," she bawled loud enough for him to hear.

She slid out from under the bed to meet face-to-face with the oily too-too wretch.

He cleaned out her room one day when Precious was at work, and when she came back she took him aside and said please not to clean out my room for I am a woman and no man is supposed to clean out my room, I am supposed to clean out my own room plus man's one too, and I have been doing it for years and take pride in keeping a clean room and don't need any man to come and sneak-clean my room behind my back when I am at work, and while she said this Precious kept a winsome smile on her face so that she wouldn't hurt his feelings.

But the next week he had cleaned out her room again, down to vacuuming the floor and dusting off her dresser, and she took him aside and this time she wore no winsome smile on her face when she said that she did not want her rass room cleaned out by any man, and though she did not use that nasty word "rass" she had sorely felt like it, and please to leave her boudoir alone for a woman's boudoir was her castle, it was the place where she reigned supreme and where man must not venture except when woman invites him in for a joint of bamboo, and she wanted to make matters so clear that never again as long as she lived would any too-too man ever attempt to clean out her room, did he understand?

That was Jamaica, Precious, said Mr. Too-too, this is America. Here men pick up and clean up after women. Men help with laundry and dishes and change diaper. In fact, when it came to wiping doo-doo baby bottom, he was foremost champion, for he himself used to wipe all the baby bottom in this family since Shirley was too busy being police and didn't like the smell of baby doo-doo, while he thought it cleared his nose better than vapor rub, and anyway he was liberated and only doing what a liberated man did in America.

Did she imprison him in America? Was she his warden? Must her room be held hostage? Must he go on a cleaning rampage through her personal possessions just because he was liberated?

Of course not, said Too-too with an ingratiating smile, and Precious felt like saying, don't smile so at me when we arguing about cleaning up my room, or so help me God I going thump you down on de spot, but she was a lady and only gritted her teeth and muttered that it struck her as no laughing matter and she was serious as a judge about not wanting man to clean her room.

"I like cleaning up your room, Precious!" Henry insisted. "Would you like a cup of coffee?"

Precious jumped like she had sat down on a bee, for she instantly recognized the tone of voice the too-too wretch was using. It was a tone that sighed, "Precious, how you so fat and juicy, eh?" and more than one man had whispered it while tamping a wriggly tongue down the shaft of her earhole and trying to coax pum-pum out of her. Indeed, the last time she had heard that tone was from Theophilus as she was helping prop up middle-aged Brutus for his weekly ride.

She glared at Henry and growled, "I box down more dan one man already dat take dat tone to me."

She jumped up and headed abruptly for her room.

"What did I say, Precious?" Too-too whined, chasing after her.

She turned to face him. They were in the narrow hallway outside her bedroom door, and he was peering at her like he was puppy dog and she was beefy bone. She felt to point a fingernail in his face and deliver stern warning but, instead, merely stomped her foot and retreated into her room.

"Precious," he scraped outside her door plaintively, "I think we're having a cultural misunderstanding!"

He washed out her drawers. It was such a shock for her to come home from work one evening and find her dirty drawers washed, rinsed, and folded neatly on her bed that if she had had dentures she might have swallowed them and choked to death. Then and there she made up her mind that she was going to thump him down on the spot, and she threw open her bedroom door and charged into the kitchen looking for the panty-rinsing wretch.

He was not in the kitchen.

"Henry!" she called, going so far as to poke her head into his bedroom, thinking that whether in kitchen, bedroom, bathroom, or laundry room, he was still getting thumped down.

He was not in the bedroom, bathroom, laundry room. He was nowhere in the house.

His car was gone and he had left her a note.

It read: *Precious: Am cooking a stew for dinner. Did the wash today, including your underthings. Hope I didn't starch the collar of your blouse too much. Ironed this morning before work, too. No rest for the wicked. See you at dinner.*

She was stalking back into her bedroom with a scowl when she heard a door slam and rushed into the kitchen with her fist doubled, ready to thump.

It was Shirley, coming home from a meeting.

They sat in the kitchen and drank coffee. Shirley saw that her mother was agitated and asked what was troubling her. Precious put the case bluntly.

"Your husband have de nerve to wash out my underwear dis morning! I going to thump him down, Shirley! So help me, I am just going to thump him down!"

Shirley frowned and looked puzzled. "Why? He didn't do a good job?"

"Do a good job?" Precious shrieked. "What business does dat man have washing out my underwear, please? What?"

"But Mummy! Is I train him, you know."

"Train him? To wash woman panty? If dis was Jamaica, de police would lock him up."

Shirley chuckled. "Mummy, you too old-fashioned. Henry is a modern American man. I put him through a long training. I discipline him de right way. Don't undo all de years of training I give dat man now."

"Tell him to leave my underwear alone if he value life and limb, to say nothing of liver, eyeball, and gall bladder!"

That night she heard Henry come home and stir about the house, picking up odds and ends discarded by the children and stacking dishes away, and she heard Shirley talking to him in the kitchen followed by anxious murmurs from Henry. A few minutes later someone tapped softly on her door and Henry whispered, "Precious?"

She lay in bed and pretended to be asleep.

"Precious!" he called again, this time more insistently. She replied with a bogus snore loud enough to inform the wretch that she was asleep.

"Is your mother sleeping?" she heard Henry ask and could not make out Shirley's garbled reply, so she gave out another thunderous snore that would have made it plain even to a deaf man that she was asleep and snoring.

"She doesn't usually go to bed this early, does she?" she heard Henry ask again.

Precious tiptoed to the door, stood silently behind it, and blasted a boar's snore through the wood. There was silence for a moment while the idiot digested the snore. Finally she heard him say in a chastened voice, "I suppose she's sleeping," and scrape away from her door as she flung another handful of bullfrog snores after the retreating brute.

"You wretch!" she carped, sneaking back to her bed. "You nearly make me blow me sinus out me nose-hole!"

The next day he was sorry.

He was sorry at breakfast when he fried her an egg even though she had already explained that there wasn't her equal in the world when it came to egg frying. He was sorry at work, for he called her between perms, she herself being off that day, to say that he was sorry. And he was sorry in the evening hours as he fluffed the cushion of her easy chair when she sat down to watch television. Ever since he recognized her habit of fluffing the cushion before she settled down to a nightly diet of American television murder shows, he had taken this preparatory fluffing upon himself as a bounden duty, and while he fluffed the cushion he explained how sorry he was that he had washed her underwear.

"Precious," he said earnestly, "I really am sorry. This is a culture difference we're encountering."

She snorted.

"Will you forgive me, Precious?" he asked, smiling in a way that God had intended only for the hyena.

She faced him squarely and stared hard at the hands hovering dangerously within fluffing distance of her cushion.

"Sit down over dere!" she ordered. "Leave me alone, Henry. I am in a bad mood."

So he sat and he gave her that look from the sofa that said, "Precious, how you so fat and juicy, eh?" and she opened her mouth as if to deny that she was fat and juicy and to assert that even if she were, it was still none of his stinking business.

"I'm telling you, Precious," he lobbed from the sofa, "we're working through culture conflict here."

Matters got worse. He mopped her floor. He cooked her a special dessert. He scoured out her tub. And he was watching her. She could tell. He was watching her because he had noticed that she was fat and juicy while his own wife was scrawny and aerobic. She couldn't really blame him for this interest, however, since everyone knew that one plump woman could drive more man crazy than a thousand female jogger, and he repeatedly told her with his tone and eyes that he had noticed how sweet and juicy she was by asking, "Precious, would you like another cup of coffee?" or, "Precious, do you want to watch another program?" or once, with special effrontery which nearly earned him a box, "Precious, tell me what your favorite dishes are and I'll cook them."

That was too much. When he approached her with this impertinence she had to swallow her bile and try to put on her best face knowing fully well that she would dead first before she allowed any man to cook special dish for her. She wouldn't even wait to dead, she'd just walk up to the empty grave and jump in without further ado.

She said with a thin smile that she had no favorite dishes.

But she must have a favorite dish, he insisted, and if she would only tell him she would make him so very happy.

But no matter how the brute begged to play cook for her, she just smiled and said she had no favorite dishes and so slowly dewormed him, for his own good, of another womanish impulse.

One night after she again repulsed his request to cook her a favorite dish she heard him pacing in the hallway. She glanced up from the television and saw that he was agitated, that he was shooting anxious glances at her such as hungry puss would give out-of-reach bird, and she felt a little sorry for him, for it was not his fault that she looked so fat and juicy, and after all, even though he was too-too he was also a man and couldn't help himself. To relieve a little of the understandable pressure she was no doubt causing, Precious excused herself and went into her bedroom.

A moment later she thought she heard him sneaking down the hall and suspected that he was outside her door peeping through the keyhole. She crept to the door and peeped back into the keyhole plugged by the blue tint of what she thought was an eye.

With a cry of indignation, she threw the door open.

The hallway was empty. A sliver of light showed under his doorway at the end of the hall. So maybe she had been imagining things, but maybe she had not, for when she peeped back through the keyhole again, she was able to glimpse the empty hallway.

The next day she scolded Shirley for leaving her husband alone too much.

Shirley shrugged wearily, for she had just returned from patrol. "Is true," she admitted. "I goin' ride him tonight."

"Ride him?"

"Yes. Ride him like a mule. Make him feel sweet."

There was a delicate pause during which Precious digested this unorthodox arrangement. "You ride *him?* He don't ride you?"

Shirley scoffed. "Ride *me?* You must want me to shoot his rass!"

So that very evening, true to her word, Shirley began to ride her too-too husband, and even with her door closed and her room down the hall, Precious could hear such disgusting unmanly groaning coming out of him that it set her teeth on edge. He didn't even know that a man was supposed to erupt in one grateful bellow when he was properly overcome by pum-pum, not moan like a draycart that wanted grease.

Really, if any man had the nerve to carry on so with her, she'd kick him straight out of her bed.

She flung the pillow off her bed, pretending that it was a too-too man bawling over pum-pum in her ears, and stepped on it so hard that feathers scattered through the room.

Henry made his move a week after Shirley had taken him on her aerobic ride.

Precious was sound asleep in her bed and peacefully dreaming, when through the mists of her dreams she thought she heard her door creak open and foot pad toward her bed, and she thought she felt an interloping batty park on the edge of her mattress, but she dismissed these queasy impressions as part of her dream and tried to roll over, when she felt a clammy hand flutter down atop her pum-pum and brush it ecstatically. She must be dreaming, she told herself sternly, or maybe Theophilus's duppy had snuck down from heaven to catch a ghostly feel-up or beg a midnight piece, so she cracked her eyes and took a frightened look.

In the dim light of the shadowy bedroom she glimpsed the too-too wretch perched on the edge of her bed and felt nasty too-too hand joyfully combing pum-pum pasture and too-too finger jumping with joy as it drilled for juice.

It was a crisis. Shirley was away on patrol, and the children were sleeping in their room down the hall. Her first impulse was to give the wretch one rass thump and pitch him headlong out the door, but then she thought that the commotion might rouse the children and cause a scandal. So she stirred and spoke with the deliberately slurred speech of one still fluttering in the swirls of a dream.

"Dis must be a dream. Whoever is in my room in my dream had better get out before I wake up and thump him down!"

"Precious," he whispered, rubbing pum-pum eagerly like he was a barber massaging a bald head with hair tonic. "Precious, is me, Henry!"

"Whoever is in my dream had better uncork pum-pum this instant before I wake up and break off his nasty finger."

She felt rueful uncorking take place and heard a little sob of bitter longing catch in the beast's throat.

"Precious! You're so wonderful!"

"Whoever is in my dream," she growled, "must have respect for mother-in-law and elder. He must get out of my room now before I wake up!"

Another snuffle of longing and regret before alien batty squeaked off her bed and was borne slowly out the door on nighttime interloping foot.

After she was sure that he was gone, Precious got up and locked her door. She returned to bed and snuggled under the blankets and reflected that strangely enough this was the first time she'd felt even grudging respect for the too-too wretch.

She sniffed and smoothed down pum-pum with a comforting rub and goodnight pat, for she felt suddenly drowsy and unable to keep her eyes open.

Nevertheless, it was too bad that she would now have to move.

And that was the last thought she had before falling into a sweet and refreshing slumber such as only mighty Brutus himself had ever been able to induce.

Chapter 10

Precious awoke the next morning with a bone in her throat. Her days at Shirley's were numbered; she would have to find somewhere else to live. It was a terrible realization to wake up to, and she would have much preferred to have opened her eyes and found no crisis waiting at her bedside, but sneaky Henry was sure to come prowling in her bedroom again. She could no longer live with him under the same roof.

"Lawd, I beg you, don't drop a tin can 'pon me head today!" she moaned her usual wakening prayer before shuffling out of bed and performing her morning wash with a dispirited air.

What would she do and where would she go? How would she explain to Shirley that she suddenly wanted to live on her own, abandoning warmth and family companionship for loneliness and empty evenings? Shirley would think her possessed.

She was brushing her hair, mulling over possibilities and feeling blue, when she was suddenly struck by her own downcast reflection. She stiffened her back and drew herself upright with dignity.

If Henry dared whisper anything romantic at breakfast, she would crack an egg over his head. She crimped her lip with determination, applied her makeup, and sallied into the kitchen.

He was waiting for her at the breakfast table.

He sneak-peeped at her over fuzzy newspaper rim. She said "Good morning" as she always did and he mumbled guiltily into the belly of the sports page. She sat down and peacefully sipped her morning tea and pretended that all was well, though tension and plots bubbled palpably between them.

Precious gazed idly at the newspaper while Henry read and her eyes fell by direction of the Holy Ghost on a want ad for a housekeeper that promised attractive salary, light work, and spacious accommodations with all found. She tried to read it by craning her neck, and as she did so Henry broke the strained silence.

"Precious," he began, still skulking behind the opened newspaper, "I just want to say—"

"I had a funny dream last night," she interrupted cheerfully. "I know it was a dream because what I dreamt couldn't happen in a million years."

"Precious, please. I know what I did was—"

"It was my bed I was in last night, my innocent bed, and I say dat what happened there was only a dream. A bad dream. Now, lend me dis piece of paper, please, to read on de toilet."

She took the want ad section from him, after thus brutally reminding him that while she no doubt appeared heavenly and beguiling, she still possessed the schoolbook twenty-three feet of bowels along with anal opening and was compelled by nature to do unseemly number two every morning, which realization she hoped would cool his ardor and bring him down to earth.

Then she sauntered off to the bathroom with the grim matronly tread of a respectable middle-aged woman about to perform her morning movement.

* * *

She had the interview for the housekeeper's job that very same day. She called the ad and spoke to a man with an accent, and after he had questioned her on the telephone, he suggested that she take a cab and be interviewed in person.

She spent an hour achieving impeccability of grooming before taking a cab to the address. The cab prowled tentatively through a neighborhood of towering mansions that peered down on the vulgar public road from behind a screen of lawns, hedges, trees, and spiked wrought-iron fences.

"This is the place," the driver said, plainly impressed, as he turned off the meter.

Precious paid the fare and stepped out, checking her footing as though she suspected that the asphalted pavement was booby-trapped. The cab drove off and she was left standing alone before a scrolled iron gate and gawking uncertainly through a spiked fence into the yard, when, suddenly, a television camera mounted on the fencepost swivelled with a watchful hum and peered down at her.

"Can I help you?" the camera asked metallically.

Precious stared up at it and stated her business in a quavering voice, feeling like an embezzler in a cathedral. Her heart began to pound with fright. The voice instructed her to stand back and the gate slid quietly open on rollers while the television camera stared morbidly after her as she entered the gravel driveway.

Precious crunched down the driveway in tottery heels, her heart beating fast, conscious that she was badly out of place, gaping at the landscaped gardens like one who had blundered into the enchanted woods of a fairy tale. From her shaky step, she might have been walking to the gallows, and the trip of her heart as she drove deeper and deeper toward the palatial house made her so breathless that she scowled and reminded herself that underfoot burrowed the same nasty freeloading worm of any tenement. She was a Christian woman destined for heaven and would not be made to feel inferior by worldly wealth, and she muttered as much to an immaculately trellised rosebush that struck an uppity and overarching pose as she hobbled past.

She was nearing the massive flanks of the mansion when she suddenly glimpsed a steamship smokestack, complete with intricate rigging and whistle, enmeshed in the web of trees that towered over the eaves behind the main house. She stopped dead in her tracks, wondering how they had managed to build a pond big enough to hold a ship, when she realized that the back of the yard bordered on water and that the ship was not cemented on the lawn but sailing past on a canal in the Atlantic.

Only one thing struck her as odd about the grounds. Scattered over the lawns and between the ornamental shrubs she thought she glimpsed some eight or nine stumps of fire hydrants. At first she thought her eyes were deceiving her and that she must be looking at plants bred by ne'er-do-well American botanists to resemble hydrants, but when she stopped and took a careful look she saw that she had made no mistake. Fire hydrants were definitely planted among the lawns and gardens; fire hydrants, without question, down even to the fluted dwarf torso and the lurid municipal red.

Well, at least if she got the job here and lived in this house she would never have to worry about fire, she smugly thought, continuing down the driveway until she found herself standing before an ornate and self-assertive front door whose knobs, embossed decorations, and leaded stained-glass exulted boastfully to the world, "I am Almighty Door."

"Lawd have mercy!" she muttered with a greater tripping of her heart as she gave Almighty Door a solid thump with her knuckles to demonstrate that man-made door could never be mightier than God-made woman.

Her interviewer was a short dapper East Indian man with the melancholy air of a clerk who'd just emerged from a gloomy matinee. He had a thick head of inky hair surgically parted in the middle and smooth cheeks inlaid with the grainy shadow of a beard. He was deferential and polite in the manner of educated East Indians and practically bowed and scraped with apology as he led her into the kitchen for the interview.

He said his name was Mannish Chaudhuri and that he was the chauffeur and general factotum for the mistress of the house, and while she was away it had fallen upon him to screen applicants for the housekeeping position and make a recommendation about their suitability. To this end, he continued, he was obliged to ask her some pertinent questions, and trusted she would not be offended by them.

Precious remarked that as a Christian woman with a vigilant soul, she was ready at this instant to appear before the Throne of Judgment, let alone before some ordinary facto—

"What you say you are again?"

"Factotum," Mannish replied primly, adding, "It is a Latin word for someone who does all."

So she said that she was ready and willing to endure any worldly interview, and to indicate as much, she interlaced her kerchief between her fingers, settled them in her lap, and put on her church-going face.

The interview went badly at first, for as Mannish brewed her a cup of tea, Precious suddenly remembered what his name reminded her of—mannish water, a clear soup boiled from goat testicles and thought to restore flagging sexual vigor in men—and struggled vainly against the impulse to smirk.

"I said something amusing?" Mannish asked, missing nothing as he returned with the steeped tea to begin the serious questioning.

Precious sternly swallowed her grin.

"We have a soup name mannish water in Jamaica," she finally said offhandedly, trying to wriggle out of it and move briskly along.

"Oh, you do. What kind of soup, if I may ask?"

"A broth."

"Oh. And how is this broth made?"

"With goat."

"With what part of goat, if I may ask?"

"The bottom part."

"Oh. Is that the part the world knows as the tail?"

Precious looked up sharply at him, determined to repel all Indian irony.

"No," she corrected boldly. "It is made of the part dat hang down underneath the male goat."

Mannish blinked as if he had suddenly been stung by a gnat in an unscratchable place. He was obviously not a man given to extreme reaction, and his blinking looked to Precious as much of a flinch as the poor soul could muster.

She pressed on with the full truth, harsh though it might be. "Men say it invigorates their nature. Personally, I don't believe it. But certain men say so."

"And it has my name. I must try this soup someday and see if it has the desired effect."

He smiled unctuously and resumed the polite questioning.

She had not been in this splendid house three minutes and already she had insulted her interviewer by telling him that he was named after goat-balls soup, Precious reflected gloomily as she fielded his questions. The opportunity for employment was obviously lost, since Mannish would certainly not want a woman around him who every time she heard or spoke his name would immediately think of ramgoat testicles bobbing in a broth. And it was perhaps this stupid blunder that led her to throw caution to the winds and open up during the interview.

She had felt bullied and put upon by the palatial driveway and grounds, and now as she sat in a kitchen so vast and ornate that its ceramic tiling flowed and silted between at least two corners—she had never before been in a kitchen to turn even one corner, much less two—she consciously decided to abandon sham and be her God-given self.

So not even halfway in the interview, Precious seemed to visibly expand and swell, and before she knew it, she was even laughing in her inimitable way at some little witticism slyly offered by Mannish. And when she laughed as she did, virtually splattering her good humor throughout the lavish kitchen, Mannish was so startled that he suspended the questioning for a moment and peeped up at her with renewed interest.

At one point, she even familiarly reached over and gave Mannish a sporting cuff on the ear, in the playful manner that Jamaicans who feel affection will genially swat an acquaintance in a bank lobby, and chuckled. For a brief instant Mannish thought he was getting his ears boxed by a Calcutta nun in primary school, but Precious was so obviously revelling in his humor that he broke down and managed at first a grin, then an outright smile, then a hearty treble laugh.

The two of them laughed without inhibition in the ornate kitchen.

Mannish regained control first, sniffed, and said, "My mother used to say that I was the least funny of all her seven children."

Precious scoffed and gave him another play-box on the ear.

"Mothers are the last to know de truth about their children, you didn't know that?"

Mannish gingerly withdrew out of cuffing range lest she shatter his eardrum with a mistimed blow.

An hour later he walked her to the front door and stood briefly with her surveying the grounds as they said goodbye.

"This place is so wonderful," Precious exclaimed, waving her hand at the landscaping splendor, "that even a dog would feel afraid to wee-wee on the grass."

Mannish chuckled. "The mistress has a beloved lapdog. And he wee-wees on this grass always. Those are his urination posts you see over there." He pointed at the stumpy fire hydrants.

Precious gaped and beamed at him with a mischievous air. "You joking again, right?"

"I am very serious," Mannish intoned grimly. "The mistress loves her dog, and when she thought he had no place suitable for alfresco urinating, she had workmen install those fake fire hydrants. She is very attached to her dog. Whoever takes this job will have to accompany Riccardo during his daily urinating promenades. It is part of the duties."

Precious shook her head emphatically. "Any dog I ever see trying to sneak a wee-wee on this lovely lawn, I'd kick all the way to Timbuktu."

Shaking hands with Mannish, she started her labored crunching down the driveway, leaving him standing before his mistress's temple, chewing pensively on his lower lip.

Chapter 11

Precious got the job. Perhaps she shouldn't have gotten the job, as things turned out, but she did get it, and for a time she was as sure as Revelations that it was the right thing to do. Nor would she learn, until many months later, that she had gotten the job over all the other applicants because in her spontaneous exuberance she had given Mannish a cuff or two on the ear and reminded him of maulings he had received from nuns at the parochial school of the childhood in India for which he was still dreadfully homesick.

She shrieked when Mannish telephoned to say that she was the one, that the mistress was still away at her Riviera chateau but that it would be best if she began at once, thus affording him the opportunity to train her in her duties so she would be thoroughly familiar with the expectations of the position and the services required by the mistress once the mistress actually arrived some weeks later. If she would therefore please to take a taxi to the house and report in three days, he would be glad to embark on what little preliminary training she might require.

When she hung up the telephone, Precious practically danced with sheer abandon and joy. Happily, the house was empty and no one was around to witness her extraordinary outburst. And after she had done with the grubby burst of ragamuffin shrieking, she trotted to her room and sat on the edge of her bed and stared at the photograph of Theophilus, who was still smiting the birdie with a hard-eye stare. Only Brutus had ever made her shriek with such wanton delight, she reflected ruefully, stroking Theophilus's image through the cold glass. She missed him. She was momentarily happy but in the long run she still missed Theophilus and now, for some peculiar reason that she couldn't explain, was dreadfully sorry that she had waited for him to be felled by death before she was willing to call game and ever-ready Brutus by his rightful name. It was such a small thing Theophilus had begged of her repeatedly, but she had stubbornly refused to do it. And yet honest Brutus used to unfailingly make her holler with delight at least once a week. Now she had nothing to holler about except for getting a job in a foreign land as a housekeeper and being separated because of it from the only people in America who loved her.

So she was happy, but she was also sad. And as people do in her contrary and somewhat wayward position, she wept a little and smiled a little and when the momentary foolishness had passed, she washed her face and applied a fresh burst of makeup and went into the kitchen to prepare dinner for the family, which she served that night along with a helping of what she thought was wonderful news.

The grandchildren did not think the news wonderful. Henry squirmed and thought it dreadful. Shirley was the only one who encouraged her mummy, for she fully understood a woman of independence and pluck wanting to establish herself in her own place and rule her own roost, be it only one room in the servant's quarters.

Cheryl-Lee flew to her side at the dinner table and begged Precious not to go since she'd only just come and who would she have to crawl under the bed and think with?

"You still crawling under de bed to think, Mummy?" asked Shirley, with raised eyebrow.

"Your father drove me to dat bad habit," fudged Precious, convinced that Shirley would understand neither her childhood fear of heaven's tin can nor her irregular conversations with Jamaican Jesus. Such inner secrets, Precious decided, were better kept from the police, even if the police happened to be one's own daughter.

Henrietta moaned that she would miss Grandma and did this mean that they would only see her once every five years as before, but Precious chuckled and said no, she would be living just around the corner and certainly would be coming by often to visit, and with that, she gave the two children a heartfelt hug.

Henry fidgeted guiltily and cleared his throat and wondered why she had to leave when they were just getting used to having her around and he certainly did not want her to go, and Precious replied with an offhand air that when it was time to come it was time to come and when it was time to go it was time to go and this was her time to go, sounding like a dyslexic tea leaf reader.

Shirley smirked and opined that Mummy was still young and attractive and in need of a man, which she certainly wouldn't find stuck here in nuclear-family suburbia.

"Your mother doesn't need a man!" Henry scoffed. "What would she do with him?"

"She would do plenty!" Shirley declared emphatically. As for Precious, she only gave the snake-in-the-grass a withering look and added nothing further to the subject.

Later that evening, as the family drifted into its customary nooks and crannies, Precious happened to encounter Henry in the hall as both were trudging toward their respective bedrooms.

"You don't have to leave because of me, Precious," he pleaded, his eyes darting up and down the hall to be sure that Shirley was not overhearing this exchange. "I'll never come into your room again."

"I am not leaving because of you," she said primly. "I am leaving because of me. It's hard on a man like you to have a woman like me around. I am just too attractive for my own good."

"Yes, you are, Precious!" he breathed eagerly, edging closer. "You really are."

"And since I have no husband anymore," she continued with a diffident wave of her hand, "yet I'm still basically a handsome woman with charm and poise, a man like you is bound to have his head turned."

"Yes, Precious!" he whimpered. "You turned my head. And I'm sorry I let you do it."

"You couldn't help yourself," she sighed heavily, conscious of bearing an unwanted burden of carnality. "But I'll be leaving in a few days and you'll be out of danger."

"I don't want to be out of danger, Precious," he begged, his eyes watering for her.

"Dry you eye! Buck up and be a man," she ordered, before he leaked eyewater over her frock. "Tomorrow, I'm going to church to pray hard and repent. Only the Lord knew what He had in mind when He put me in this position."

She would have given more suggestions, practical advice even about how he could, with hard work and application, make himself over into a man, but she had nothing to work with but a panty-rinsing husk, and the job, given the brief time left, would be simply impossible.

She shrugged and headed toward her room. He paused at the end of the hall and whispered, "Precious?"

"What?" she asked from her doorway, the hall stretching rigidly between them.

"I forgive you."

"Thank you," she said with an accepting nod.

It was only after she was in her room, undressed and lying in bed, that she began feeling squeamish about the conversation she had had in the hall with the too-too wretch, which she thought had bordered on unseemly intimacy. Moreover, she really couldn't believe that the brute had had the nerve to forgive her, as if she was the one that had puss-sneaked into his room to feel him up, and the more she thought about the gall of this man to forgive her the more she felt like tramping down the hall and dropping one good thump on the wretch in his sleep. She also found it hard to believe that she had had the nerve to admit to the too-too brute that she was still young and handsome, even though that was plainly obvious to the whole world. Really, what could have possessed her, she wondered, to hold such a slack conversation with him?

Then she realized with a start that tonight was a Saturday night, the very night when Brutus duppy would most likely be prowling about her bed, whispering his week's worth of pent-up nastiness into her unfenced earhole.

"Brutus!" she hissed to the empty room. "Go 'way! You dead and gone!"

And that night, for the first time since she had been in America, Precious wept with longing over Theophilus.

Two days later she moved into the maid's quarters of the Fort Lauderdale mansion and became its housekeeper.

PART 2

Chapter 12

Since the days when cave-dwelling women first had to contend with bumptious stalagmites, every house has had the perverse desire to bully a new female occupant. If Precious had come to the mansion as its mistress rather than as its maid, she would have shown who was boss in the usual female way, by making mansion feel the whip of renovation and carpentry, the boot heel of paint-brush, the spur of shifted sofa and newly hung curtains. But coming as a lowly maid, she felt powerless and cowed when she crossed the mansion's threshold carrying her two battered suitcases.

As if revelling in advantage, the mansion greeted Precious with an arrogant sneer of wealth and comfort, baring twenty-two bedrooms, four drawing rooms, swimming pool that could land a seaplane, and bathrooms enough to empty every running stomach at a Boy Scout jamboree. It reeled off acres of wall, plastered thick with animal pictures, and endless hallways that swirled a creamy wash of ceramic tile into opulent rooms.

Whirling inside her brain as Precious meekly followed Mannish on the tour throughout the mansion and gardens was a dust storm of schoolday modifiers such as "gargantuan," "spacious," "immense," "massive," and "colossal."

"You could keep a John Crow inside here," Precious muttered, trying vainly to clear her brain of the flying debris of unruly adjectives as it strained to cope with the magnificence underfoot, "and he wouldn't even know he was in a house."

"Oh, really," said Mannish. "And what is a John Crow, if I may ask?"

"Dat what we call buzzard in Jamaica," Precious said lamely, conscious that in her cowed state she was perilously close to misspeaking. "He could fly around inside all day and never miss de outdoors. But, of course," she added to make it clear that she was no ornithological fool, "John Crow wouldn't be happy inside without dead body to eat."

"It is a big house," Mannish conceded coolly. "And although the mistress is an animal lover, as you can tell from these pictures on the walls, I do not believe she would consent to an interior buzzard."

"I only mean to say," Precious stumbled, "dat de house big. It well big."

Her own quarters, discreetly in the rear of the mansion, consisted of a spacious bedroom furnished with a dresser and side tables with a telephone. Her sitting room sported a color television and a radio, her bathroom an enormous marble tub. Above her bed hung pictures of what Precious at first thought were rats, but Mannish said were mink.

"I trust that you will be comfortable here," Mannish murmured, discreetly leaving her to unpack and settle.

A few minutes later she heard him drive away in the Rolls Royce.

She unpacked and tentatively applied the whip to mansion rump. She stripped the pictures off the walls and stacked them neatly in a bottom drawer. Mink or no mink, they still resembled brown rat to her, and she would not stomach rat picture hanging over her head. She moved a chair from one corner to another and rearranged the sofa and side table in her sitting room. These were only tiny shifts, but they showed her as a woman accustomed to rulership over house.

She was sitting on the edge of the bed, catching her breath, when the phone on the table began to bark like a watchdog at a postman. Stupefied, Precious stared as it barked once, then twice, then a third time, before it dawned on her that the bark was a kind of demented American ring. She picked up the phone and timidly whispered, "Hello?" and an accented voice asked, "Is Mannish there, please?"

Precious said he was not and the voice chuckled even though she'd said nothing funny and asked her please to tell Mannish that his cousin called. She replaced the receiver on the cradle and took an awed breath.

"Me God! A barking phone. What will dey think of next?"

When Mannish returned Precious mentioned the barking phone and the message from the cousin. Mannish explained that all the phones in the house were specially made to bark, some to "Bow wow," others to "Woof woof" or "Arf arf." Hers, as she had no doubt found out, was an "Arf arf" poodle phone. Precious wondered if she could throw a switch on the phone to remove the poodle and restore a normal ring, but Mannish said no, all the phones in the house were designed to bark.

"All de phones bark?" Precious repeated.

"Every one, without exception," Mannish confirmed.

"Phone not supposed to bark," Jamaican Jesus warned in the back of her head.

During her first days of mansion life Precious was as idle as a pickpocket among nudists.

'She had thought she would be working her fingers to the bone cleaning out mansion, but a maid service came in that very next morning and left every room sparkling and smelling like a freshly sprayed armpit. That same afternoon the yard work was done by a grinning Chinyman who rode his mower over the lawn, clipped the bushes, sprayed the roses, and edged the circular driveway. When he was finished the outdoors looked as though the Chinyman had shrink-wrapped it in cellophane. Later, two strapping young men with chemicals arrived and made the pool sparkle. Moreover, Precious soon discovered that with the mistress away not a soul visited the mansion. She did not even have to cook since all Mannish wanted to do every night for dinner was to drive out in the Rolls Royce and buy hamburgers.

Mannish had nothing for her to do. He himself had nothing to do. Every morning he woke up at around 10 o'clock and pointed the satellite dish at the heavens and tapped into an Indian program, which he settled before the television to watch as he drank breakfast tea. When Precious asked him what she should do, he waved airily and said that she should get accustomed to the house and achieve peace of mind, for they were on holiday until the mistress and Riccardo returned. When the mistress returned Precious would have plenty to do, not to worry.

But she could not help but worry, for without regular household duties she felt out of place like a puss at high tea.

She wandered into the gardens to pick flowers and felt foreign. She sat on the edge of the furry lawn abutting the intracoastal canal and felt alien. People riding past in motorboats and yachts stared at her and made her feel peculiar. Sitting on the deck around the pool, she felt as unwelcome as urban bullfrog. She would drift back into the house, hoping to chat with Mannish, to find him engrossed in his Indian program where everyone spoke incomprehensible Coolie. She would sometimes sit down nearby and watch, but the sound of nothing but Coolie talk soon made her feel so queasy that she would have to retire to the bathroom.

But the bathroom awed her. The living room cowed her. The kitchen humbled her. The barking phones made her heart jump. And everywhere she stepped, animal pictures gawked at her from the walls.

Three days this bullying went on, with mansion doing its best to prove that it was the belly and she the tapeworm.

Precious began retreating under her bed to think.

She was hiding there on this third evening, asking herself what she could do to keep from being cowed by mansion, when it struck her that what she needed was a cobweb.

To find and clean out a cobweb would prove that mansion was human with a dirty batty. She felt giddy at the prospect of the wiping that must surely follow.

But where would she find a cobweb inside a sparkling mansion? She squirted out from under the bed and set out on a cobweb hunt.

Through twenty-one of the twenty-two bedrooms she stalked, searching diligently for a cobweb. From room to room she went, crouching under bed and looking behind toilet. There was no cobweb to be found. Finally, she came to the last unsearched room and found the door mysteriously bolted.

Disappointed, she slunk back into the cavernous drawing room to find Mannish curled up in a stupor on the couch, still watching Indian program.

Returning to her room, Precious briefly considered smuggling a cobweb from Shirley's house before deciding that a CIA cobweb would not give the satisfaction of one directly from mansion's own nasty batty.

Her head aswirl with thoughts and schemes, she then did what any Christian woman in her position would do: She said a prayer asking Jesus (the Jamaican) please to deliver unto her a cobweb.

And Jesus heard.

For within the hour, as she was preparing to brush her teeth, she spotted a minuscule cobweb dangling from the toilet lock-off valve near the floor.

With a noisy hallelujah, she jumped up, pulled on her bathrobe, and rushed into the living room to find Mannish dozing on the couch. She roused him indignantly, announcing that she wished him to witness what nastiness she had found in her bathroom, and the poor Indian chauffeur, groggy after hours of watching television, shambled after her into the bathroom, where he stared with thickening stupefaction as she pointed to a frail strand of glossy cobweb dangling from the lock-off valve seconds before attacking it with domestic viciousness.

Mannish peered at her as she wiped triumphantly, and after a long embarrassing pause during which he recalled the name of the continent his foot presently walked on, he finally summoned up the presence of mind to mutter respectfully, "You are the cleanest woman I have ever met in my entire life."

Precious slept that night the refreshing sleep of the innocent. And when she awoke next morning, she was impossibly pleased with herself.

Mansion had a dirty batty; she had wiped it.

Her rulership was now established.

But there was still nothing to do. She began to seriously wonder why she had been hired. Then it hit her. A man who would employ a woman for $250 a week with all found and give her nothing to do could only be out for one thing. One night she would wake up out of a deep sleep to find the Indian wriggling naked atop her slumbering belly, bawling for moonlight pum-pum.

Naturally she would thump him down and chuck him straight out the door.

She pondered further. If only Mannish were not a sneaky Coolie, she would certainly find him attractive. But she would never forget how a Coolie boy with whom she had been playing the fishing-in-drawers game had once dropped a sand crab down her panties. The crab had seized the rim of her pum-pum with its claw, and Precious had had to hurriedly rip off her panties before the beast mistook itself and went scuttling down the wrong hide-out hole, exposing her to medical mortification before the village nurse.

Now that it was clearer to her why she had been hired, she felt considerably better. She looked forward to the moment when moody Mannish would make his move so she could box his face, clear the air between them, and set events into motion. Night after night as she settled into her bed with a sigh, she could even feel the tingle in her palm from smiting Coolie cheek. Some nights she even lay in bed and practiced boxing down a Coolie on the tiled floor.

But after the third week when he failed to make his move, Precious became testy and quarrelsome, wondering again what she had done to earn the lovely room with a private bath in the back of the house, and if the brute had gone to all this trouble just for a little pum-pum, why he wasn't man enough to come and beg for it honorably instead of sneaking around like a chartered accountant?

If it was one thing Precious couldn't stand, it was man circling her like crow, especially after getting used to forthright Brutus who, during his frisky years, would sometimes vulgarly jump right out of his tent flap like he was at a Revival meeting. But Mannish made no move and did not come creeping into her bedroom at night, and during daylight hours was as polite as church usher during collection. All he did was watch television and gobble down hamburgers. All she did was loll about the house, doing a little occasional feather-dusting and fixing the odd sandwich. And nearly every night she phoned up Shirley and the grandchildren and pretended to be busy and happy with mansion life, while all along she was wondering what on earth she was doing to earn her money.

She did savor a quiet satisfaction, however, from inviting Shirley and the family to visit her at the mansion, with Mannish's permission, and one Sunday afternoon they arrived when the chauffeur was discreetly away, and she drew respectful "Oohs" and "Aahs" out of them as she led them on a tour through the household splendor. Shirley asked question after question, pawed brocade fabric and felt up crystal bauble, while the two children were so impressed with the barking phones that they suspended their usual monkeyshines and acted as if they were in a museum.

"This is America for you, Mummy!" Shirley marvelled in a hushed voice. "Only four months in America, and already you living in a mansion complete with swimming pool and barking phone!"

"She's only the maid, Shirley," Henry grumbled, shuffling surlily behind them.

"Shut up about maid!" Shirley snapped at him over her shoulder. "She still living in a mansion! Where your mansion?"

"I am not a maid," Precious corrected Henry primly. "My title is factotum."

"See!" Shirley crowed. "She's factotum, not maid. Congratulations, you hear, Mummy! I knew you would do well in America."

And she waved her hand with a lavish sweep that deposited all the mansion glory that unfolded around them at her mummy's immigrant feet. Precious beamed with inexpressible pleasure.

After the family had gone home, Precious retreated wearily into her own rooms to savor the glow of melting-pot triumph. Theophilus glowered disapprovingly at her from the dresser, and since there was a chance sneaky Mannish might come tiptoeing into her room tonight, Precious thought it best to spare her dead husband the trauma of witnessing Coolie romancing.

She turned his portrait gently so Theophilus could glower to his heart's content at the wall and went to bed wondering if tonight was the night she would wake up to find a Coolie eelet wriggling atop her bellybutton.

Then suddenly the holiday was over, and nearly four weeks of getting fat in a mansion crashed to an abrupt end.

One evening she suddenly found that all traces of meat had mysteriously disappeared from the refrigerator and the pantry, which now bulged sanctimoniously with cheese, beans, yogurt, and green leafy vegetables. She went looking for Mannish and found him before the television, gourmandizing a giant hamburger. When she asked him, pray, what happened to the ham in the refrigerator, Mannish sheepishly explained that the mistress was a vegetarian who went berserk at the sight of meat, and that he was enjoying his last hamburger since she was returning tomorrow in her private jet and until she left would starve him on nothing but beans and cheese and dairy products.

"I always become constipated on such a diet," he said gloomily. Then, waving the hamburger defiantly, he added,

"This is possibly my last dead cow on the premises for two or three months."

"Dead cow?"

"That is what the mistress calls hamburgers," he said grumpily, chomping shamelessly on the carcass wedged in a sesame seed bun. Precious reflected inwardly that if a woman wanted to call a hamburger a dead cow, that was her prerogative no matter what any carping Coolie said. What she found utterly baffling was that the mistress would be arriving in her own personal jet plane without media coverage. You would think that such a wonder would merit at least as much attention as a mass murder.

Wiping his mouth, Mannish interrupted her daydream by saying that he hoped everything was spick and span for the mistress's arrival. Precious assured him that everything was most certainly spick and span.

To prove it to him, she led him through the house, pointing out spickness and spanness. He nodded and sniffed and looked pleased and rubbed his hands together like he was nervous, and Precious got the impression he was dying to tell her something.

They ended up in the drawing room where Mannish poured her a glass of wine and sank down to his elbows in a plush couch.

"Precious," he began somberly, "now we must earn our salary. And there is something about the mistress that I must tell you."

His manner was so glum that Precious braced herself for news about syphilis, goiter, hunchback, or hideous deformity.

"You must understand, Precious," he said crisply, "that Americans are not like we immigrants. It happens that they have everything while our own countries have nothing."

annish padded back out of the room, closing the door
ly after him.

hat is all for tonight, Precious," he said suavely, coming
to where she stood gaping like she was painted on a
my shell. "See? Was that so bad?"

he dog kicks?" Precious asked, following the Indian down
allway into the living room, which seemed to her to have
enly and inexplicably shrunk with the arrival of the mistress.

his is America, Precious," Mannish assured her smoothly,
g her on the arm. "Sometimes dogs kick in America."

n Jamaica only donkey and mule kick," Precious
bled, feeling stupid.

ndeed so. That is another difference between the two
res. It is as I explained last night."

st night.

st night there had been trauma, scene, and serious
estic brouhaha. When she had found out that she had
hired as dog maid, Precious had carried on and made
thing of an unladylike stink, especially since she had
nced herself that the sneaky Indian had hired her for
pum. Mannish did not know what pum-pum was and
ous had had to clumsily enlighten him, using gestures and
emisms and biblical phrases such as when a man "knew a
an" like Solomon and David and other patriarchs had
n thousands of earthly concubines before going off to
en to have knowledge of the female angel legions.
nish still did not get what Precious thought she had been
for, forcing her to grope for metaphor and simile until he
y saw the light. Of course, he assured her quickly when he
ed her meaning, that was also definitely on his mind when
d selected her, and upon hearing this snide confession,
ous slapped his pudgy cheek with a sharp box for making

"I beg your pardon," Precious interrupted stiffly, her
patriotism aroused. "Maybe where you come from you have
nothing but holy cow, but Jamaica—"

Mannish cut her off impatiently. "Your Jamaica does not
have everything. My India does not have everything. Here, in
this house, in this country, the people are used to having
everything. This is what makes them eccentric."

Precious felt her argumentative dander rising at this forward
Coolie presuming to lecture her about her own country. But
Mannish raised his hand like a bishop and squashed her with
an upheld palm. "I will show you what I mean," he said
decisively. "Please follow me without questioning."

He trotted down the warren of corridors until he came to the
one room whose door had remained closed ever since Precious
had been in the mansion.

Pausing until she was right at his side, he unlocked the door
and turned on the light to reveal a spacious bedroom with an
enormous king-size bed, a room that first seemed to Precious,
whose eyes were now hardened to mansion splendors, no better
than others of its brethren on either side of the corridor, when
her darting gaze was drawn irresistibly to a bizarre assemblage
of paintings and pictures hanging on the wall.

The bottom half of one wall was thick with pictures of fire
hydrants, tree trunks, street signs, country stumps, and
construction posts. Most peculiarly, all the pictures and
paintings were hung at nearly ground level, no higher than
three feet from the floor, while the upper stretches of the walls
were conspicuously bare.

Precious's chin had dropped down to her neck bone. Her mouth
gaped and her stupefied tongue briefly and visibly wallowed.
Mannish observed her reaction and looked pleased. "This," he

announced with triumph, "is Riccardo's bedroom. These are his favorite pictures. Please. Just observe while I finish my point."

He opened the bathroom door to reveal, to a gasp of astonishment from Precious, that the shower stall had been converted to a sandbox in which was planted, with ominous perpendicularity that spoke volumes about spendthrift carpentry and misguided plumbing, a fire hydrant.

"And this," Mannish said smoothly, "is Riccardo's bathroom. This is his indoor hydrant."

"A dog live in dis room?" Precious whispered, stepping slowly through the room as if she was treading atop a fresh grave.

"Yes," Mannish replied. He whipped off the bedspread to reveal a custom-fitted sheet gaily imprinted with endless patterns of bones. "And he prefers his cotton sheets to be changed every day."

"Changed every day?" Precious echoed dimly, moving across the room to gape at the bone pictures. "Den, pray tell me, who is de dog maid in charge of changing bone sheet every day?"

Mannish peered hard at her, his sanded cheek darting with a noiseless, guilty twitch.

Revelation burst on Precious's senses like a thunderclap.

"You brute," she gasped accusingly, "is not pum-pum you hire me for! Is dog maid!"

Chapter 13

The mistress came home late that night, thre[...] at Precious who was wedged in a corner tin[...] and groaned that she couldn't cope.

"A new maid, Mannish!" she shrieked [...] cope with this tonight. I just can't cope!"

Riccardo trotted in behind the mistres[...] Precious, bared his teeth and gave a menac[...] understood to be Dog for he couldn't cope, [...]

"Mannish," the mistress commanded bef[...] her room, "Riccardo sleeps in his own room[...] kicks too much in his sleep. Last night he ne[...] of my own bed."

Then she was gone, leaving Mannish b[...] soothing, "Very good, ma'am."

The Indian led Riccardo down the [...] bedroom door, and escorted him inside wh[...] with astonishment from her post in the corr[...] dog turned and shot a smutty glance at Prec[...] off the ground where dog eye beaded and [...] sockets of dog head, and the only other hum[...] remember ever giving her such a nasty look [...] on her wedding day.

her wait a whole unrequited month to be awakened by a naked Coolie wriggling atop her slumbering belly.

He took the blow, winced, and bowed. "Of course," he said humbly, "I deserve that slap. It was definitely your body I was after. I am so sorry."

"You liar!" Precious screamed. "Is dog maid you wanted! Well, if you think for a minute that this woman is going to be maid to some mangy dog . . ."

"I assure you, Precious," Mannish said gravely, "the dog has no mange."

Precious was not pacified.

"Giving dog a room with bone picture hanging off de wall and fire hydrant in de bathroom!" she shrieked. "What kind of sick mind would do such a thing?"

"Not an Indian mind, Precious. It is an American mind. Indians do not worship dog. It is here in America that they think that the dog is god. Indeed, 'Dog' spelled backward in American is 'God.'"

Precious had never considered this point before, and although her rage was still bubbling, she was momentarily floored by this profound observation.

Mannish had taken advantage of the lull to lead her back into the living room and ply her with another glass of wine while he explained that he had not meant to mislead her, that from the start he had been drawn to her obvious voluptuousness . . .

"You want another box?" Precious asked belligerently.

Certainly not. That was the last thing he wanted on this earth. What he most desperately wanted was for Precious to stay on the job and not walk out as she had seemed poised to do a moment ago. The mistress owned five houses in three countries. She stayed here with Riccardo only a few months out of the year. Sometimes she was gone for three, four months, during which there would be nothing for them to do but enjoy the luxury, to live in the house as if it were their own, and all Precious would be required to do for the short time the mistress was in residence was to take care of Riccardo, who was at heart a good dog, seldom bad-tempered or surly.

Precious stared stonily at him while he babbled explanations and begged her to stay. Of course, he did not know that she had to stay, that she simply couldn't return to Shirley's house. He could not know, moreover, that mansion living was beginning to sweet Precious down to the bone; that already she had grown to love the way eyes peered enviously at her as she stepped with a flourish through mansion gate, walking with the proprietary tread of a woman who regularly skimmed fashion magazine on mansion toilet; that Shirley's praise of her accomplishments had gone to her head; that she was prepared to fight to keep her foot in mansion door. But she still pretended that her mind was set in cement and that she was leaving.

In the face of her apparent obstinacy, Mannish got agitated and performed a jerky orbit around the spacious drawing room. He stopped after his third revolution, peered down at Precious, and begged her to stay and save him from arrest for cannibalizing the dog.

Precious nearly jumped out of her skin with terror. "Say what?"

He was on his knees, begging, his black eyes rolling in a bed of angst and fury.

"Precious," he gasped, "if you leave, I will kill that dog and curry him. I know that I will do this horrible thing because I almost did it once. I hate that dog so very much that I want desperately to cook and eat him."

"Merciful heavens!" Precious yelped. "Stop you damn foolishness. Why you talking such rubbish?"

"It is not rubbish. That dog humiliates me and makes me feel wretched. If you do not stay, I swear I will curry the bugger. Then I will go to jail and not fulfill my destiny with Beulah."

"What? What you talking about, eh?"

Mannish sighed, took a slow turn around the room, and confessed in a solemn voice. "Some years ago, I cheated a man of some camels. It is my karma to repay the debt by suffering under American Beulah. She is out there waiting for me. And when she comes, I will have no choice but to be her husband."

"I didn't understand a word of that!" Precious squawked, pointing an accusing finger at the wretch's befuddling mouth. "You thief a camel from a man so now you must marry some American woman name Beulah? What kind of madhouse is dis? What does dis have to do with eating de dog?"

"It is my destiny to suffer at the hands of American Beulah or my soul will not grow. I am destined to breed Beulah of two children. She will use superior argumentation to make me get a vasectomy. At her hands, I will suffer a lifetime of washing dishes, and mowing grasses, and cleaning toilets. And in the end, she will still not appreciate my virtues."

"Be a man and kick her in her bottom," Precious advised before adding, with a squeal of exasperation, "What does dis mad story have to do with eating de dog?"

He put his finger to his lips and begged her in sign language not to shout. Drawing near, he whispered conspiratorially into her earhole, tickling her lobe with his moustache, "I am only working here until I meet Beulah, then I will leave and marry her and begin my reparations. But if I lose control and eat the dog, they will put me in an American prison and I will have to waste another lifetime before I can repay the debt in regards to the camel. That is why you must stay and help me, Precious. You will not feel a similar temptation to eat the dog."

"I should say not!"

"It is just that I have suffered so much humiliation from that dog that I cannot lose the idea that one day I might forget myself and eat him. Americans do not like it when Indians migrate to their shores and eat their dogs. Will you stay, please? Once the mistress leaves, we will have the house altogether to ourselves again. We can go on Sunday outings in the Rolls."

Precious thought for a moment before hitting on a practical suggestion. "Why don't you just go to de man you thief de camel from and pay him what you owe him and be done with it? Then you wouldn't have to worry about American Beulah."

"I can't. It happened seven hundred years ago."

"Heavenly Kingdom!"

"Precious, you must believe me!"

Mannish was down on his knees again, trying anew to clamber up her leg.

Precious blew a deep cleansing breath. Already she had $1,000 of American money in her bank account—every penny of her salary for a month. There was absolutely no danger that she would forget her upbringing and eat this or any other dog. She was beginning to grasp that the Indian was not only sneaky but also very possibly out of his head.

She looked at the beseeching chauffeur down on his knees before her and was certain that his thick greasy hair was daubing pomade all over the hem of her frock.

"I will stay," she finally conceded, ungluing his head from her frock front. "I will take care of de dog. Only promise me one thing," she warned, pointing her finger between his eyes.

"Promise me I won't wake up one night to find you naked on me belly."

"Precious, I would never do such a thing without your permission."

"Good! Now, beg you two aspirin. I have a beast of a headache."

"Certainly!"

Mannish jumped to his feet and raced to the back bathroom and returned with a tumbler of water and some pills.

She swallowed the aspirin and drank the water.

"And if I'm in charge of dat dog," she warned, handing the empty tumbler back to Mannish, "he better not forget himself with me, either. Where I come from, a dog is a dog is a dog, and dat is de end of it."

Mannish smiled impulsively and tried to give her a kiss. She dodged his swooping lips and pushed him gently away. Then she icily said goodnight and headed for her room, her wounded pride at least temporarily assuaged by the rebuff.

Chapter 14

Early the next morning, Riccardo ambled out of the French doors onto the lawn, giving Precious her first good daytime look at the pampered brute.

He was the size and shape of an obese baby warthog, with a blunt and bevelled snout and a stumpy body trimmed along the underbelly with a flounce of gray fur. His legs seemed comically stubby for his rotund body, as did his thuggish head buttoned taut at the snout by a chitinous black nose. Tasselled with hairy tufts and antlered with sharpened ears, the dog strutted onto the lawn with the prudish, self-important trot of a centipede.

In the garden Riccardo did what dogs customarily do to perpendicular objects: He raised his leg and sprayed them with fastidious little squirts.

"Enough of de eternal wee-weeing," Precious scolded. "Come, back to de house. I see you mistress on de porch."

She turned to head for the porch but the dog stubbornly refused to follow, making his way to another row of stumpy hydrants. Precious trailed after him, clucking, "Stop de foolishness, dog! You think you's a walking watering can?"

The dog, however, continued willfully on his self-appointed rounds. When he was finally satiated, he kicked up a few clods of grass and trotted briskly across the lawn toward the porch where the mistress sat, wearing a pink peignoir and clutching her head.

"Who invented the jet plane?" the mistress groaned as Precious ambled within earshot.

"De jet plane, mum?" Precious replied, stunned at the abrupt question.

"Yes," the mistress sighed. "Who in his right mind would invent such a torture chamber? And why do we give in to it? Why did we not fight back? What was your name again?"

Mannish padded onto the veranda, carrying a silver salver on which were balanced a coffee pot and a cup. "Her name is Precious, ma'am." To Precious he added suavely as he poured the coffee, "The mistress is suffering from jet lag."

The mistress clutched her head between both hands as if to dramatize her pitiful suffering. Riccardo jumped onto her lap and wound into a furry pile atop her crotch.

"How's my baby?" cooed the mistress. Riccardo answered by burrowing his nose into her crotch and taking a deep draft.

The mistress giggled and stroked her dog, who responded by streaking her face with his slimy red tongue.

"I am a woman who has been dissected by aviation, Precious, or whatever your name is," the mistress continued languidly, after she had been thoroughly moistened by dog mouthwater. "My left side is in Paris. My right side is in London. My stomach is in Bangor. But where is my liver? And where is my heart? And where are my kidneys? Can you tell me?"

"All within de skin, mum," Precious replied scripturally. "Thanks to the plan of God, skin holds us together and keeps everything safely inside. Unless, of course, a madman come and hack you to pieces and fling a piece of you here and another piece dere. Odderwise, where you find skin, inside you will always find organs, all sides, and de eternal soul."

The mistress heaved a piteous groan and winced, "Mannish, vivisectionist gore so early in the morning?"

"Oh, no, mum! Is de work of God, ma'am," Precious assured her, interpreting "vivisectionist gore" as the materialist's rebuttal of Divine Plan.

"Mannish! Otherworldly propaganda before 10 o'clock?"

Mannish made as if to interpose with soothing explanation, when Riccardo unkinked like an awakened snake, leapt down from the mistress's lap, sidled up to Precious, and spontaneously pumped two strawfuls of yellow wee-wee over her brown shoes.

"De dog wee-wee all over me new shoe!" Precious shrieked with heartfelt horror and disgust, raising her leaking foot to stomp the beast.

Mannish was at Precious's side in a blink, gripping her elbow in a vice.

"Precious!" he hissed urgently into her earhole.

"Wee-wee dripping between me toe!" Precious howled another blast of revulsion, shaking her feet to drip-dry her toes of dog urine.

"It is not wee-wee!" the mistress said sternly, jumping up and giving Precious a disciplinary shake. "It is love!"

Floored by this revelation, Precious stared down at her splattered feet with momentary bewilderment.

"Don't be so speciest!" the mistress scolded shrilly, piercing Precious's eyes with her stare. "Riccardo has no arms for hugging. He has no fingers for caressing. He can only claim you as his own and express his love for you through urination."

"He has claimed me for his own, too, Precious," Mannish added grimly, "three times. But it took him nearly a year before he did so the first time."

"This is what is so remarkable!" the mistress gushed. "Riccardo has fallen in love with you within a matter of hours. Go over and pat him on the head and show that you understand the sign he has given you, that you accept his love."

Precious was staring confusedly from the mistress to her shoe so rapidly that she felt a muscle spasm in the back of her neck.

Mannish interposed artfully, "However, I think Precious should first take time to cleanse her feet."

The mistress shrugged. "Another opportunity for rapprochement between the species lost to petty human hygiene," she said with palpable disgust. "Go wash your feet."

She slumped wearily on the lounge, grimacing with a look of dark disappointment.

With Mannish at her side gripping her elbow and helping her along, Precious limped toward her room on tippy toe to prevent her foot bottom from being marinated in dog urine.

"Mannish," she whispered as soon as they were out of earshot of the porch, "am I mad? Is not wee-wee de dog just spray on me foot?"

"It was indubitably wee-wee," the factotum confirmed.

"For a little bit I thought I was outta me head. After forty-seven years of life, you just want to believe you can tell de difference between love and wee-wee, you know?"

"Your senses are perfectly sound," Mannish assured her, giving her arm an encouraging pat as he helped her down the hallway toward her quarters.

"What dat she call me, 'speciest'? What dat mean?"

"It means you look at the world as a human being does."

"So how should I look at it, pray?"

"Like a dog."

"I must drag myself down to de level of dog and look 'pon de world like it fill up with hydrant and bone? For what purpose, please? Dog must raise himself up to *my* level!"

Precious urgently grabbed and held the factotum in her doorway before he could glide off.

"Mannish, if dat dog claim me again, I goin' kill him dead, so help me."

"It is over, Precious," Mannish assured her with another soothing pat. "He has already claimed you. Wash and all will be well."

Precious sat on the edge of her tub and washed her feet with scalding water, scrubbing between the toes with a washrag, soaping down instep, insole, and the balls of her feet repeatedly until she was certain that all trace of dog bodily fluid had been cleansed from her person.

She dried off her foot, threw the befouled shoes into the garbage, and returned to the veranda, where, at the mistress's insistence, she patted Riccardo gingerly on the head to acknowledge the token of liquefied affection he had earlier dumped over her shoes, although the mistress mourned it would have been far better if Precious had reciprocated on the spot, for patting the dog now was like being told, "I love you," and then replying a month later, "I love you, too." Nevertheless, Riccardo seemed to understand for he wagged his tail and, as she patted his head, licked Precious plentifully over hand and foot—an experience she likened to being blotted with an uncooked oyster.

"You are a member of this family now, Precious," the mistress beamed, after Precious had weathered the dog lathering. "Riccardo is an infallible judge of human character. Three days before the market crashed in October 1987, he bit my Merrill Lynch broker. I sold all my stock immediately and made a $25 million profit. I knew that Riccardo never bites without good reason. I told my friends, 'Riccardo bit my broker, sell your stock immediately.' They all laughed at me. They don't laugh anymore. People do learn."

"Yes, mum," Precious muttered, reluctant to assert what every Christian believer already knew—that the Bible soundly refutes dog bite as a source of true prophecy.

"Sit down and tell me about yourself," the mistress invited, waving Precious to a chair.

Precious sat down on the veranda, after first peering cautiously at the dog who was still curled up contentedly atop his mistress's lap. She took a breath and began, starting her narration with her birth in Clarendon one rainy evening in the days when the one parish midwife still rode a donkey. The midwife had to ford two swollen rivers before she could reach the scene of Precious's birth, and the backward donkey was just getting his front foot damp in river water when the mistress turned glassy-eyed and dozed off. Precious's head had not yet crowned in the birth canal before the first blast of snoring sounded. Mannish appeared on the veranda and nodded approvingly at Precious, signalling her to keep talking.

Riccardo, however, listened with a impertinent expression riveted on his snout, ignoring Precious's occasional scowls that were intended to get him to caulk his ears and stop the snooping since a woman's personal biography was none of any dog's damn business.

Chapter 15

The mistress didn't look enough like a millionaire to suit Precious, who had expected a flabby old woman with a greedy face soiled by money and stomped on by bird-foot wrinkles. Instead, what she disappointingly got was a middle-aged blond woman whose frame was fashionably strung with modern-day sinew and gristle but whose posture bore a pronounced tilt to the right, possibly, Precious surmised, the result of being knocked out of plumb by a primary schoolteacher's box and never quite straightening. This constant incline had cocked the mistress's left eyebrow, giving it the arched look of being jammed on an unfired wink, and clouded her face with an expression of unappetizing quizzicality.

According to Mannish, who told Precious gossipy stories at nights when they shared a few moments of peace and quiet, the mistress had made her money the old-fashioned way: through death and widowhood. She had been married to a man who had invented a useful valve. Precious had only a vague idea of what a valve was and did, but Mannish explained to her that the principle behind a valve was regulation. This appealed to the disciplinary Christian in Precious, who was of the opinion that lack of personal regulation in the world was the chief cause of worldwide smut. Man and woman alike these days could not regulate bad habit, vice, misguided opinion, and wayward appetite, she lectured Mannish, who listened with his inscrutable Coolie face while Precious digressed with a little uplifting postprandial rant in the kitchen.

"Personally, if a woman make her money off regulation, I am for dat. Regulation is important to everyone who professes to be upright and moral."

"That, however, is not the sort of regulation that a valve performs," Mannish insisted. "Valves regulate flow. Flow of water. Flow of oil. Flow of liquids and gases. Valves have nothing to do with moral regulation."

"I am aware of dat, Mister Mannish," Precious replied sharply. "I am not stupid. I'm just saying dat lack of regulation is de blight on today's youth."

Mannish did not know what was the blight on today's youth; he only knew that the mistress's husband had invented a valve originally intended for toilets, but it was such a valuable device that its use quickly spread to oil and chemical pumps. The husband patented the device, licensed its manufacture, and then was good enough to drop dead, leaving all his worldly wealth to his bereaved wife.

"But she was not much bereaved," Mannish added, snippily, "which is why you cannot find a single picture of the dead gentleman in this house."

Precious rose stoutly to the mistress's defense.

"Dat's why I would never marry a Coolie, because you are a people who want woman to sit 'round and do nothing but bawl out her heart and eyewater for you when you dead. Some of you even burn de widow when you dead, as if a woman was nothing but firewood. When you dead, man, you dead. Take it like a man! If you live a wholesome life, you gone to heaven. If you did not live a wholesome life, all de bawling in de world can't reclaim you from de fiery pit."

"I am only telling you what I know about the mistress," Mannish insisted, blinking at this harsh criticism. "I know when I am dead that Beulah will cremate me, even though it is against my wishes. But that is the price I must pay if my soul is to grow."

"De everlasting Beulah again!" groaned Precious. "Go on with de story."

"There is little else to tell. Except that the mistress has made many fortunes several times over. Riccardo is her financial advisor. If she is considering an investment, she will invite the broker for a visit. If Riccardo bites him, she will not invest. But if he urinates on the broker's shoe, she invests a lot. She says that the dog is a prophet who has never been wrong."

"De dog is a false prophet," Precious pronounced grimly.

Mannish said he knew nothing about prophets, he only knew that Riccardo had never bitten any broker whose schemes made money. And he had yet to urinate over the shoes of one whose projects had failed.

"How can anybody in deir right mind invest thousands over dog wee-wee?"

"Millions, Precious," Mannish murmured. "Millions."

A slab of mansion stillness intruded on their discussion, which they were holding in the cathedral kitchen. Three hallways and a living room deep into the house, as they spoke quietly, the investment dog was snoring on a cotton bone sheet, while his mistress had gone out for a nighttime romp with a date.

"A madhouse, dis America, you know dat, Mannish!" Precious finally observed, shaking her head with Christian bewilderment. "You ever consider dat dis is a country where everybody mad at de same time, and because of dat, it seem like nobody mad, when in fact, everybody mad?"

Mannish said he hadn't looked at it that way. He raised his hand to voice philosophical objection when the alarm went off and they saw in the security monitor that a car had pulled into the driveway and that the mistress was being ushered to the front door by her escort.

Precious went to help the mistress prepare for bed and found her sitting sourpussed at her vanity, pawing at her limp blond hair with a brush.

"What's the use of men, Precious?" she asked bluntly.

"We need dem to have children, mum," Precious ventured.

"That's no good. I've never wanted children."

Precious considered a secondary use for man.

"Dey are idlers, drunkards, and sinners whose souls need saving, mum. All a Christian woman need is to save one of de brutes' soul and heaven will be her reward."

"Religious bunk. Men have no souls."

The mistress prowled agitatedly around the enormous manless room, looping the perimeter of the gigantic bed where she slept alone every night, looking exasperated and vexed.

"For once in my life, I just want to meet a man who's more of a man than I am. You know what I mean?"

"But dat applies to every old negar man off de street, mum!" Precious protested.

The mistress did not quite get "old negar man," but the drift was plain enough to merit rebuttal.

"It does not. It applies to none of the men I have ever known," she snapped, glaring. "Like tonight. I went out with Harold. He tries to screw me. I say 'No,' and you know what he did? He started to cry. Can you imagine that?"

Precious could sympathize with this outrage, which reminded her of the too-too wretch. She sneered without mercy, "I'd box his face and say, 'Who you bawling to, wretch! Hush up and get outta me sight!' Den de next Sunday, I'd drag him into church."

Mistress Lucy looked startled. "Why didn't I do that?" she exclaimed enviously, clouting herself on her forehead with an open palm at her gross omission. "I'll call him on his car phone."

She rushed to the telephone, dialed, and putting on a bogus smile and manner, purred, "Harold, turn around and come back at once. I want to continue our conversation . . . Yes, yes. I said turn back."

Hanging up, the mistress threw on her housecoat and rushed into the living room and out the front door to ambush Harold while Precious, who had only been playing the battle-axe, followed with a gaping mouth, fretting about revocation of her green card for inciting assault. "But I also say, Mistress Lucy," she sputtered, "dat I'd carry him to church de next Sunday!"

"*You* carry him to church," the mistress threw scornfully over her shoulder from her shadowy ambuscade. "I'm just going to slap his face silly."

They were interrupted by the distinctive crunching of tires in the driveway and the garish creaminess of headlights spilling over the dark landscaped grounds.

Precious slunk in the shadows of the living room, unsure of what to do next. She was weighing rushing down the hallway to Mannish's room and pleading for the factotum's intervention when the front door suddenly banged shut, the mistress stalked past, and Harold's car roared away.

Poking her head timidly through the ajar bedroom door at the end of the long hallway, Precious spied the mistress standing under the pearly glow of the bathroom light. She was soaking her right hand under a rushing tap.

"That was a wonderful suggestion, Precious!" she chortled triumphantly. "Go get Riccardo for me, will you please? I want some company in my bed tonight. What a refreshing whack that was! Keep coming up with such wonderful ideas and I'll give you a raise."

Grumbling under her breath about being innocent in the vicious assault on Harold, Precious went to the dog's bedroom where she roused him snarling from his slumber atop the cotton bone sheets and coaxed him into the mistress's bedroom. The dog immediately jumped up and snuggled beside the mistress on the bed, who engulfed him in a bosomy hug.

"You're more man than a thousand men," she cooed at the dog, who slushed her face repeatedly, greasing it with dog mouthwater.

Later that night Precious went under her bed to talk to Jamaican Jesus and explain that she had not meant for the mistress to attack Harold, that she had only been using a manner and tone of speaking that Jamaican wives habitually use on their own verandas to cuss and berate worthless husbands, and that she didn't feel it was fair that she should be charged with inciting assault and possibly get an undeserved singeing of her bosom if she should die tonight. (Precious always imagined with a shudder that if ever she got a broiling on hell's spit, which she was determined she never would, it would be atop her tender, swollen breasts that malicious demons would gleefully plop glowing rivets.) Jesus said he quite understood, for he had sat on the same verandas night after night and heard plenty plenty Jamaican old wife rant about what they intended to do to the worthless brute, once the worthless brute finally crawled out of the rum bar and staggered home, without ever giving the brute more than hot cocoa and a tongue-lashing. However, Jesus counselled against talk that advocated violence because he could see that Americans were plainly a people who took everything at face value and didn't understand Jamaican veranda chat. Precious said, yes, she saw that herself, though she refrained from the criticism that here was evidently a serious flaw in the creation.

Nevertheless, Precious sighed, as she settled wearily under her sheets, she still didn't understand how a woman could let a dog sleep with her and couldn't even visualize the way the dog had licked up the mistress's face without a spasm of disgust.

Jesus said he didn't understand it, either. It was a mystery to him. Americans were a strange and perplexing people about their dogs. Sometimes he felt like just turning around and going back home. Precious said she felt that way every day. And she would, too, as soon as she made a little more money and didn't have to return to wallow penniless among peak.

How much money did she have saved up now? Jesus wondered, and Precious told him that she had just exceeded $1,600, which made Jesus whistle once he did the arithmetic on conversion into Jamaican dollars at the black-market rate.

Just before dozing off, Precious muttered a sincere prayer of thanks that her Jesus was a native Jamaican who understood her ways. God only knew what she would do had he been a foreigner.

Chapter 16

Mistress Lucy awoke in her ornate bedroom and began to think fretfully about the woeful history of protoplasm. It was a subject she often thought about as she crawled through the crack between dreaming and waking, and this morning she came back to it anew as to a persistent toothache. She understood with grim certainty how she had come to live upon this earth but still found it philosophically bracing to occasionally relive the harsh facts.

In the morning of her earth nothing existed but rain, mist, and stone. Then one day a disgruntled stone took up foot and walked; soon it grew a mouth and began to eat next-door stone, which grew a voicebox and began to bellow. After eons of such rampant eating and bellowing, a stone named Mozart began composing symphonies, another named Leopold crowned himself King of Bohemia, and the incidental tomfoolery of ancestral stone had become recorded human history. To Mistress Lucy's way of thinking, that she walked on two foot and owned a Rolls Royce was nothing but an accidental cosmic perk. Flesh was still the child of stone whether the flesh had been pulped into a dog that barked at the moon or a preacher who shrieked on a pulpit.

Mistress Lucy passionately believed that justice and love should flow between all fellow creatures; that monkey should sit at the dining room table with the family and not be left to eat alone in the dingy kitchen like a poor relation from the country; that people should not be so small-minded as to prefer speech to barking just because speech was comprehensible and barking was not, the blame being on the speciest school curriculum with its senseless craze for the human alphabet; that mistress of the house should not lord it over mongoose and worm as if home ownership entitled her to assume airs over the rest of creation; and that man should not be so vain as to think himself the only son of stone in the cosmos to whom woman might be attracted.

Given this cosmic philosophy, the mistress could not have been more utterly at odds with Precious if they had been rival capitalists playing at monopoly, for they were two women with vastly different outlooks and life ambitions. Mistress Lucy longed to consort with her fellow creatures under the common sun and save them from cruel human depredations, while Precious aspired to be the first Jamaican-born archangel and, if such lofty goal proved beyond the reach of humble colonial circumstance and island birth, to be appointed guardian angel for some drunken man whose soul she could curb of craven gluttony by whispering preachment in his ears as the brute caroused.

In spite of their differences, Mistress Lucy was soon freely confiding her man problems to Precious during intense mistress-to-maid chats. As a Jamaican Christian woman used to the management of sinners in trousers, as some sisters of her congregation had nicknamed men, Precious regarded herself as an expert in manhood and capable of grappling with almost anything that herd of hard-of-hearing beasts could provoke.

But the mistress had her own bizarre ethic about man, which proved a source of mystery and wonder to Precious, who did not understand, for example, why the mistress lost respect for Richard, a strapping investment banker, after discovering that she was the better water-skier. Nor did she approve when she overheard the mistress tell the dog that he was more of a man than Richard. Such treatment, Precious was grimly convinced, would only give the dog airs.

Argument naturally followed. One particularly bitter row began when Peter, another date, became sick in the door of an airplane and chickened out of skydiving with the mistress as he had promised. The mistress jumped by herself and heaped scorn and contempt on him afterwards, again telling the dog in front of Precious the lie that he was more man than cowardly Peter.

Precious was moved to gainsay.

"Mistress Lucy," she said boldly, "you know what dat dog would do if you put parachute on him and push him to de open door of a plane? He would bite you."

The mistress looked momentarily startled, then replied heatedly, "Riccardo is a brave dog! He would jump!"

Precious scoffed. "You wouldn't even get de parachute on de dog without a biting."

"I know Riccardo better than you! He would jump! He wouldn't bite. Why am I taking part in this silly argument?"

Just then Mannish ghosted around the corner, observed female row in progress, and tried to slink off. The mistress, however, beckoned him over, installed him as judge for this argument, and asked his opinion: Would the dog bite if asked to skydive or would he reveal the courage and loyalty of his nature and jump?

"It depends on what the dog was before he incarnated as a dog," Mannish adjudicated gravely. "If he was a parachutist in a former life he would recall the experience and jump. Otherwise, I am of the opinion he would offer resistance."

"Former life!" jeered Precious. "Nothing in scripture say dat man get reborn as dog!"

The mistress agreed. "There's no former life. There's no future life. The dog would jump. This is my house, my dog. You are my employees. I expect philosophical unity under my own roof. The dog would jump. Right, Mannish?"

Mannish's head bobbed up and down in a chicken-hearted nod. "If you say he would jump, I am also of the mind that he would jump."

"Right, Precious?"

"There is earth, mum, and rules of earth which all must obey. But there is also heaven, and rules of heaven, which none must disobey. De dog would bite."

Mistress Lucy became shrill. "To say that the dog would jump is against your religion?"

Mannish tried to defuse tension with a joke. "I believe Precious was a snapping turtle in a former life."

"I have a good mind to dismiss you right now—contradicting me about the nature of my dog. Who do you think you are? This is *my* dog! I know what he would do! He would jump!"

"Bite, mum."

Mistress Lucy frothed with anger over this unreasonable opposition. Finally she snarled, "This is what you get from employing Third World help," and stomped off with Riccardo cradled in her arms.

"Precious," Mannish whispered urgently, "what harm is there in saying that the dog would jump?"

"Because beast of the field must never be exalted over man. De dog would bite. And next time you come tell me any of you rudeness 'bout me was a snapping turtle in anodder life, you goin' get a box, for I know who my modder was, and my grandmodder, and my great-grandmodder, and for your information, not a one of dem was a turtle, Mister Mannish Chaudhuri!"

Then she flounced angrily out of the room.

The mistress suffered an ongoing, inordinate, excessive dotage on animals. She felt sorrow for every conceivable beast and creature on earth, some of which Precious had not even known existed. Once when Precious was putting on her only silken shawl, the mistress paused on her way out the door to explain that the silk had been spun by slave worms. Precious blinked and said she didn't understand. The mistress explained that silkworms were enslaved in the Orient and compelled to weave fingers to the bone day and night by wicked overseers, and anyone who bought and wore silk contributed to international worm enslavement.

The mistress departed, leaving Precious standing before a mirror feeling guilty. She was about to take off the shawl and burn it when she realized that whatever happened in the Orient was between Chinyman and worm and none of a Jamaican's business. She had an additional flicker of insight: A worm was a worm, and the whole race of them were nothing but malingerers who would benefit from the discipline of hard work. Moreover, when she came to think of it, which worm had fingers to weave to the bone day and night? She would wear her shawl and hold up her head when she did it.

And she did wear her shawl one time after that encounter, drawing from the mistress a single sour comment: "Slave fabric."

After that, Precious locked the shawl away in her suitcase, where it stayed until she returned to Jamaica.

Wildebeest migration was the next issue the mistress, in her animal dotage, used to browbeat Precious.

Precious had stumbled into the mistress's bedroom and found her staring morosely at the ceiling.

"I'm thinking about the wildebeest migration, Precious. This month they're dying by the thousands. Drought. Disease. Predators. Barbed wire. Poachers. They fall off cliffs. They drown in rivers. They die in wildfires. Believe me, you would not want to be a wildebeest this month."

Not having the foggiest idea what a wildebeest was, Precious's first impulse was to declare that she was proud to be Jamaican and let it go at that, but instincts told her that such an answer would not satisfy. Fumbling for words, she decided to seek the anchorage of scripture. "God will provide, mum," she said.

"God!" the mistress shrieked. "Who do you think made the wildebeest migrate? Do you think any free, sensible wildebeest would want to trek hundreds of miles across the African plains in the blazing sun to be eaten, broiled, drowned, scavenged, and torn from limb to limb? Who do you think gave the wildebeest this insane obsession to trek hundreds of miles to its death? God is not an animal lover! God would not be welcome in the ASPCA!"

With a curt "Come with me," the mistress marched stupefied Precious into the sun room, where she put on a video on the wildebeest migration and forced her to watch.

Once she saw that the mistress had been fretting herself over nothing but a big-headed, horned African mule, Precious was unaffected by the program, which showed wildebeest falling prey to disease, flood, lions, wild dogs, alligators, hyenas, and leopards. However, as she watched with an occasional fatalistic shrug, she felt a stab of resentment at having Africa so blatantly thrown up in her face. She cared no more about ugly wildebeest than she did about unruly Africa, and she resented the implication that just because her skin was brown, between her and that dark continent ran an invisible umbilical cord.

"Now what do you think of your God?" the mistress challenged when the video was over.

Precious balked, mansion or no mansion, flung caution to the wind, and replied sharply, "God don't have nothing to do with wildebeest. My God business only with souls. And nothing with horn on him head have a soul."

"Why, you're nothing but a meat-eater!" the mistress spat with venom.

"I am a Jamaican Christian, mum."

"It's the same thing!"

"Not all we Jamaican Christians eat meat, mum!" Precious maintained stoutly. "I know a parson in St. Elizabeth who eat only rice and peas."

But the mistress was gone and the unfinished argument left wriggling on mansion floor among the trimmings of marble, crystal, and brocade, while wildebeest migration tape rewound on the VCR with a nonsectarian whir.

The mistress had never in her life met a denser and more obdurate mind than was encased in the cranium of this galling Jamaican maid, and she was determined to liberate it of narrowness, cultural imbecility, and human-centered vanity — or so she angrily announced to Mannish that morning. Once she had worked such liberation, she would exact delicious vengeance by firing the Jamaican. Nothing else would appease her unbounded rage.

Mannish suavely reminded the mistress that Riccardo loved Precious so much as to have claimed her within one day, an unheard of endorsement. The mistress paced agitatedly and said yes, yes, she knew all that and she respected Riccardo's judgment, but being in daily contact with a hardened meat-eater was driving her nuts. She had never before met such a wasted mind. It had been stewed in superstition, saturated fat, bogus theology, and rioting free radicals. Inadequacies of nutrition, education, and threadbare culture had conspired to destroy and lay waste its every cell. Membranes had been plucked and stripped bare by ignorance, neurons flayed by repeated religious homilies. Inside that cranium slushed nothing but cholesterol, goo, and petroleum jelly.

"Plus, Riccardo could be wrong! Have you thought of that?"

"He was right about IBM," Mannish inserted smoothly.

The mistress looked sorely oppressed.

The next day after this conversation, Mannish warned Precious that she was upsetting the mistress with her stubbornness. "You are driving the mistress mad, is what I am trying to say."

"She driving me mad, too! Have de nerve to come show me tape 'bout wildebeest migration and Africa! What those things have to do with me, anyway? I am a Jamaican Christian!"

Mannish sighed and said he understood, and that the mistress missed the point altogether about the wildebeest herd, which was nothing more than a parking lot for souls who wanted to reincarnate on the hoof rather than come back as humans and face such modern dilemmas as drive-by shooting and runaway inflation.

Precious stared at him. "De wildebeest, a parking lot? What is de matter with you, eh? Where you get dese ideas from? Souls are not cars and draycarts! Souls don't need a parking. And if dey needed a parking, de Lord will park dem in heavenly garage, not in some big-headed ole African mule."

"That is one way to look at life, heaven, and wildebeest. There are others ways, also."

"But I have no fear about Mistress Lucy, for my Jesus will subdue her. Empires, monarchs, and kingdoms must bow down, and so will this American millionaire with a jet plane."

"Why must you insist that she bow down? If she wishes to remain upright, permit her to remain upright. You are too strict with this business of bowing down."

"She must bow because she is human, not God. And all must bow to God."

The factotum sighed. "Soon now she will leave and take the beastly dog with her. Then we will have a holiday. We can eat hamburger and steak every night. It is so little to ask for life in a wonderful mansion."

Precious admitted that she was fast reaching the stage where beans and cheese and yogurt and salad greens and sprouts were maddening her brain. Last night she had almost taken a bus to buy a hamburger. "I'm at de point where, so help me, even a wildebeest look tasty."

Peering over his shoulder with a nervous shudder, Mannish shushed her savagely.

Chapter 17

Now that the mistress was in residence the mansion glittered and rang regularly with fêtes and parties, which Precious came to relish. She delighted in the crunch of limousines cruising up the gravel driveway and her ear had become so sensitive that it could distinguish authentic Rolls Royce crunch from the bogus crunch of upstart Mercedes-Benz, frowzy Acura, to say nothing of slum-dwelling Cadillac.

Many of these fêtes and gala functions were hosted by the mistress in the honor of needy animals. There was a benefit for elephants; a ball for the white rhinoceros; a concert for the California condor; a rock and roll party for the snail darter; a dinner for the monarch butterfly and various formal teas and assorted soirées for alligators, lions, Bengal tigers, cheetahs, and hyenas. Precious learned to cook what the mistress termed "cruelty-free" dishes, vegetarian meals such as melon soup, ravioli stuffed with ratatouille, meatless black bean stew, carrot and asparagus mousse, and tofu ice cream.

At these functions there was no leather worn, no pigskin, fur, silk, or animal pelt or skin of any kind. Shoes were made of synthetic materials or rubber and guests regularly attended with their pets. Some Rovers and Fidos sported sweaters and vests, and Precious saw at least one Fifi adorned with a diamond choker. Weaving in and out of the assembled guests, serving cocktails and snacks, Precious overheard many highbrow conversations that she remembered long afterwards.

She overheard arguments over whether animal experimenters deserved to be shot, hanged, or parboiled; and one memorable dispute about whether vintage Rolls Royces should remain cowed or be decowed. Those who clung to the opinion that the Rolls Royce with its leather upholstery should remain cowed argued vehemently that since the cow was already dead and stripped of its hide for the upholstery, it would be a further waste to decow the Rolls by removing the leather and giving it a decent Christian burial as proposed by the decowing side. Others just as passionately countered that they simply could not ride around in a Rolls Royce with a clear conscience knowing that the automobile seats had cost innocent cows their lives.

"I decowed my Rolls the day after I bought it," Precious overheard an earnest gray-haired gentleman say primly to a matronly lady. "I had the leather stripped off and replaced with synthetic fabric. I could never drive around knowing that my back was touching an animal corpse!"

"But the cow is already dead!" the matron cried. "At least you give the cow a posthumous reason for dying by not decowing the seats. Otherwise, why did the cow die?"

"Let's ask the meat-eater," the dignified man suggested, using the nickname the company had dubbed Precious, who had been unofficially adopted as a mock mascot of the movement and was winding her way through the crowd carrying a salver of bite-sized raw vegetables.

Precious rather enjoyed this attention from such an elegant throng and made no attempt to dodge or repudiate her meat-eating reputation. When asked for her opinion on various ethical questions, she always delivered brisk judgments in a categorical tone. Here and now, for example, she declared that she thought decowing of Rolls Royces a criminal waste. If the cow was already dead and turned into a car seat, she thought it futility itself to try to turn the car seat back into a cow. As far as she could see, the decowing movement had been cooked up by grave-diggers to drum up business by encouraging wholesale burial of Rolls Royce seats. The debaters listened and pursed their lips after she had uttered this opinion and drifted out of sight, and one of them remarked that for a meat-eater whose brain had been corroded by animal fat she was surprisingly sensible.

During these meetings Precious also got to see some of the videotape commercials made for the animal rights movement to discourage meat-eating, the wearing of hides and pelts, and the upholstering of sofas and car seats with sheepskin and leather. One commercial made with funds provided by the mistress showed a man with mouth agape about to chomp into a hamburger when suddenly the patty was transmogrified into a miniature cow which raised one slice of the bun off his bloody head, begged the diner's pardon, and said politely, "Excuse me, you may think I'm a Big Mac, but in fact, I'm actually the corpse of a dead animal."

The cow then respectfully narrated the story of its short and violent life, beginning with memories of idyllic calfhood on the ranch when he cavorted in the company of his protective bull father and doting heifer mother; romped with his brother and sister cows, all of whom had since been slaughtered; loved to breathe the clean air of the mountain pastures and frolic among blossoming meadows. He told of the day when he was herded into a cramped truck and unceremoniously dumped into a slaughter yard in the company of his two sisters and a brother, all of whom milled around anxiously wondering what fate lay in store for them. With somber music playing in the background, the cow choked up as it related how he saw a man pole-axe his favorite sister and tried desperately to intervene but was himself set upon by butchers and felled by savage clubbing; how his carcass was dismembered and hung on a rotating belt, passing cutting stations where men and women with knives and saws reduced him from a recognizable life form to a bloody miscellany of chops, roasts, steaks, loins, stew meat, and hamburger, until he wound up in his present sorry state, smashed into a hapless patty, charred and grilled, slabbed between bun slices, and crowned with a corona of chopped onions and relish.

"Go ahead," the cow gulped with a sob of sorrow and resignation, crawling back between the buns and lowering the lid atop his pole-axed head, "bite me! Enjoy your supper. Have a nice life. Mine is over, because of you."

When the lights came back on, the audience applauded wildly and called rapturously for the mistress to come forward and take a bow.

Mistress Lucy curtsied and made a fiery speech vowing to see that commercial run on television even if she had to personally buy a station just for that purpose. Everyone roared approval and many in the audience jumped to their feet and begged her to run for governor. Just then Precious re-entered bearing a tray of cocktails, and a man in the back of the room cried, in good-natured raillery, "Boo the Jamaican meat-eater!" and a rush of taunting boos and jeers, more drunken than spiteful, crackled through the room.

Riccardo, trotting in her wake, snapped at one man who blasted a raucous Bronx-cheer at her temple as Precious walked past serving drinks with stoical dignity in the storm of pagan scoffing.

"Dog," Precious scolded over her shoulder, "you is not me husband or me watchman! If face need boxing, I will box it! I don't need no dog to bite foot over me!"

Nevertheless, the heedless dog still lunged at the man and gave him an impertinent and unauthorized nip in Precious's name.

A few days after this party Precious accompanied Mistress Lucy on a visit to the animal graveyard where Barbarosa, the mistress's last dog, was buried. Precious sat in the front seat of the Rolls, wrestling with Riccardo in her lap, who kept trying to spear his nose deep into her crotch. After one particularly ugly spasm, during which she clamped her hand over the dog's muzzle and aimed its probing nose at Mannish's batty flattened out against the decowed upholstery, muttering inwardly to herself, *You want to smell something, smell a Coolie batty!* the mistress asked to have her pet. With a sigh of gratitude, Precious handed over Riccardo, who burrowed into the mistress's lap, sniffing swinishly.

The cemetery itself made Precious shudder like she had laid eyes on wicked Babylon, for she saw the hand of grotesque mockery everywhere in the lush and rolling lawns grinning with memorial to *Rover*, cenotaph to *Fido*, gravestone to *Spot*, mausoleum to *Spike*. Some of the memorials had the statue of a leaping dog on the roof, with the name of the buried dog engraved in marble. Others sported statuary of fawning dog, fetching dog, barking dog, romping dog, all petrified in the death-grip of burial stone. The mistress trotted determinedly down a footpath until she came to the memorial to Barbarosa, an imposing block of rectangular stone with the usual masonry dog romping on its top.

While the mistress murmured to her deceased dog, Precious and Mannish stood somberly in the shadow of a nearby granite tomb atop of which another stone dog looked up from a marble bone. Precious read the gilded inscription chiselled into monument:

> *Monument erected to* Ranger, *who fell overboard somewhere in the South Pacific off the motor yacht* Laffer, *on 24th September, 1982. Sadly missed by Mommy.*

"De dog drop off de boat," Precious whispered to the factotum, who was dug into the topsoil against the frenzied struggles of leashed Riccardo, driven berserk at the endless vistas of unstained monuments and tombstones. Mannish nudged her in the ribs as she was about to add that if she owned a motorboat no dog on earth would ever set foot 'pon it so there would be no dog to drop off and feed the fish, and she peered and saw that the mistress was leaning against the stone monument, quietly weeping.

On their way home, the mistress asked Precious for a Christian opinion of what happened to a dog when it died. Before she had seen the mistress weep over Barbarosa, Precious would have crisply answered, "Evaporation." But now she did not have the heart to expose the grieving mistress to the brutal truth of scripture. She swallowed and said through her teeth that only the Almighty knew. The mistress opined, after a thoughtful pause, that she felt quite sure in her heart that all flesh was doomed to rot into the nothingness of dust. But she was also convinced that if it were improbably otherwise, Barbarosa would be with her in the afterlife, as would Riccardo, as would her childhood hamster and every other pet she had ever known and loved. Precious told herself grimly that in the heaven to which Jamaican Christians were bound she was certain she would not buck up White Dog and Red Dog, for in the promised land no woman would ever have to worry about fending off Spot, Fido, or Rover who wanted to jump up all over her clean frock and nasty it up with pawprint and dog slobber. Maybe there was an American section, however, where dogs and hamsters were kept in clean cages. She did not know. God moved in mysterious ways. It was not for her to question, only to give praise, obey, and reap salvation.

The decowed Rolls Royce hummed its way back to the mansion, each of its occupants cocooned in their own thoughts. Curled up atop the mistress's lap, his nose dug into her crotch and sniffing its vapors, Riccardo fell into a drugged sleep as if he had huffed a pot of glue.

Mannish, however, when they dissected the visit, saw nothing disgusting about the cemetery, and he revealed this opinion privately to Precious later. He admitted feeling that way the first time. But like everything else, he had gotten over the initial horror and now regarded these trips as comedy.

"Americans are mad," Precious kept insisting, while Mannish equivocated against this extreme view. Finally, he allowed, "It is healthy and necessary for them to be mad to permit opportunity for recent immigrants, for between a poor sane immigrant and a rich mad American, there is no true competition. My cousin, for instance, has started a business to freeze-dry dead animals. He is assured of prosperity."

"Freeze-dry dead animals? How he do dat?"

"He has a special chamber into which he puts the dead animal for some weeks. It removes all the moisture and leaves the animal lightweight and lifelike. After freeze-drying, you can carry the animal everywhere you go, on vacation in your suitcase, if you wish. You can place him on display on the bureau of your hotel or motel room. Since he is waterproof, you can also take a bath or a wash with him. He is perfectly preserved, like a statue."

"Freeze-drying animals! What next, oh Father Above? What is dis, if not American lunacy? As soon as I have enough money, I am leaving dis place and returning home."

Mannish shook his head gloomily. "I will never go home. I will die here. Beulah will cremate me. I will leave Beulah with two children for American culture to madden. It is a heavy price to pay for stealing five camels. But God is nothing else if not thorough."

Precious bristled at upcoming blasphemy. "God is good and kind," she declared piously. "He loves us all."

"Yes, perhaps so, but he is also thorough. For example, there was a soul who was afraid of water. So what does God do to teach him not to be afraid of water? He places him aboard an Eskimo kayak, causes it to capsize, and drowns him. Then he reincarnates him in Russia, and drowns him again, this time in a river. He brings the poor frightened wretch back again, puts him aboard the *Titanic*, and drowns him a third time. He then puts him aboard a German submarine during World War II, causes it to be depth-charged, and drowns him two hundred feet below the surface. He has drowned this poor man, who is afraid of water, fifty-four times. He has drowned him in rivers, streams, brooks, seas, oceans, bathtubs, and vats. Once he drowned him as an infant in a toilet bowl. Why? Because he wants to teach this soul to be unafraid of water. I think that is too thorough."

Precious sat gaping through this heresy. When she finally stirred, it was with a subterranean bellow of indignation from deep inside her diaphragm, the same resonant place out of which "Rock of Ages" unfailingly blasted. "First of all," she snapped, "tell me how you know all dis about dis man."

"This man was my brother. He drowned when we were children swimming in the Krishna River. A holy man told me at the funeral. He says that my brother will be reborn in California for additional drowning in a hot tub. He says the only way God will cease drowning my brother is when my brother's soul loses its fear of water."

"Who created your brother?" Precious bellowed like she was witnessing in church. "Who blow de spark of life into dat worthless soul? You? De Prime Minister of India? It was God! If He create de soul, He have every right to drown it. Drown me, oh Lord," Precious howled to the ceiling, arms outstretched wide enough to engulf crystal chandelier. "Drown me not fifty-four times, but three thousand score. Drown me again and again, for when I walk wid de Lord, I have no fear."

"He won't drown you," Mannish replied coolly. "He only drowns those who are afraid of water. This is altogether too thorough."

Later that night Precious asked Jamaican Jesus what he thought of the factotum's opinion. Jesus scoffed and said she shouldn't listen to Coolie man, because they were harum-scarum and had no brain. Nevertheless, Precious was not appeased.

It was a good thing for that Mannish that she was not God, she grumbled as she snuggled down to sleep, for if she had her own way she would drown the blasphemous wretch this very night in his own mouthwater to teach him the difference between Almighty God and an earthbound Coolie.

Chapter 18

Precious was under strict orders to bathe the dog three times a week, and the mistress would occasionally comb through his stubby body from head to toe and raise the dickens if she found even a comatose flea clinging half-dead to a tuck of fat. She would stomp into the presence of Precious and fling the flea on a nearby table with a sneering, "Look at what I found on Riccardo!" as if she expected flea deadweight to shatter the glass tabletop and make Precious's malingering eardrums ring. After two such admonishing incidents, Precious began to carefully bathe the dog.

During the first days of bathing, Precious tried to maintain a carefree banter with the animal, but was soon exhausted in her search for appropriate topics. Then she had an inspiration: While bathing the dog, she would recite scripture. Since dog couldn't tell scripture from a jingle, if she used a conversational rather than a homiletic tone, dog soothing was bound to result while giving her upliftment from the recitation. So the next time Precious knelt down to scrub the dog, she began reciting the Old Testament book of Leviticus, which she knew by heart. The dog whimpered and stood stock still, hypnotized by prophecy.

Precious murmured, "These are the living things which ye may eat among all the beasts that are on the earth. Whatsoever parteth the hoof, and is cloven-footed, and cheweth the cud, among the beasts, that may ye eat. Nevertheless, these shall ye not eat of them that chew the cud, or of them that part the hoof: The camel, because he cheweth the cud but parteth not the hoof, he is unclean unto you."

Leviticus or not, Precious still didn't like the idea of having to bathe a dog hood. Every dog she'd ever known had always bathed his own hood with his nasty tongue, and she didn't see why this dog had to be any different. But the mistress was emphatic that the bathing of the dog must include a good scrubbing and rinsing of its hood, and Precious carried out lawful command. But she was never so out of order as to recite scripture while bathing such a worldly part.

Anyone standing outside the door of the bathroom would have heard muttering of scripture followed by an interval of grim silence punctuated only by the sound of sullen scrubbing, a loud wheeze of relief, and then rinsing. And occasionally the eavesdropper might even hear a fervent "Thank God!" breathed behind the closed door, signifying that the bathing of dog hood was once again accomplished.

So the bathing was going well and had even taken on an encouraging Sunday piety. But one day during his bath the dog rolled moonstruck eye at Precious and proceeded to unreel several inches of raw hood meat as if he expected a Jamaican Christian to rinse that, too. Precious scowled. "Draw in you hood, dog!" she commanded in her best headmistress tone. The dog growled a defiant "nay"; hood oozed out of its sling, bucked, and began bobbing head gravely like a chanting bishop.

Precious immediately ceased all washing and scripture reciting and sat down on the bathroom floor. Averting her eyes, she began to hum a hymn, intending to crush nasty dog hood with a psalm.

The first verse of "Rock of Ages" caused hood to tremble and shrink, Precious noted smugly, since lewdness must ever withdraw before the hymns of heaven. She had observed the same effect on rural libertines who would sometimes parade into church hoping to corrupt a sister, only to suffer smiting by the Holy Ghost. She remembered one wooer who had strutted in boastily and who ended up fluttering between the pews, babbling in tongues, and eventually becoming an elder. It was the same with earthly dog—the beast was discovering that hood did not hold sway over grace. Soon she would have him barking in tongues. She took in a deep breath, ready to bellow out "Nearer My God to Thee," when she observed that not even a wink of hood meat showed.

Precious clambered up from the floor and resumed the rinsing with a grim satisfaction. She could have gloated, and had the dog been a man, she certainly would have closed out the incident with a moral. However, she would not waste Truth on a dog, so she merely muttered the countrywoman's triumphant "Ahoa!" and got on with the bath.

But the victory was short-lived, and the bathing became more and more of a struggle. The dog persisted in exposing himself to her, though she repeatedly made clear her preference for a hood-free tub. Singing it down had become impossible. After that first time, not even the Mormon Tabernacle Choir hymning at point-blank range in the dog's ear could have shrunk his hood. Precious steeled herself to endure the provocation.

One day as Precious was drying him off, the dog exploded in a lecherous growl, seized her right leg with its front paws, and began to violently chisel her shinbone with its pointed hood. Precious shrieked bloody murder and tried to scramble down the corridor, but the lustful dog hung onto her leg and savagely pumped.

"Dog grinding me foot!" Precious bellowed loud enough to bring down the gates of heaven.

Mannish burst out of his room and bounded along the hall toward them. Mistress Lucy peered down the hallway at the commotion.

With a violent kick, Precious flung the animal off her leg and scrabbled atop the dining room table.

Mistress Lucy rushed into the room. "What did you do to Riccardo?" she snapped, eyes blazing as she knelt beside the dog, groggy from being hurled against the wall.

"De dog try to grind me foot!" Precious babbled, nearly hysterical with disgust.

"What's wrong with that? The greatest love a male can give a female is to fertilize her!"

"Breed me with puppy," blubbered Precious, shuddering at the appalling prospect.

"Impossible!" the mistress raged, as she cuddled Riccardo protectively. "Screwing another species is the best birth control in the world! Riccardo loves you, Precious! Can't you get that through your stupid head? You could have hurt Riccardo!"

"Riccardo could have grind me!"

Mistress Lucy gently picked up her dog, slathered a row of wet kisses up and down the lining of his dripping jaw, and started down the corridor with the animal slung over her shoulder. Riccardo peered longingly at Precious from his shoulder perch and whimpered.

"Tomorrow, I am gone from dis nasty place!" Precious screeched. "Away from dat nasty beast dat have de nerve to try and grind a Christian woman!"

"Go tonight," the mistress spat, disappearing down the corridor. "Don't wait until tomorrow."

"Can I help you off the table, Precious?" Mannish asked, extending his hand.

"No!" Precious snapped. "You would sit by and let a dog grind me and do nothing! You're a worthless man!"

She had a good mind to kick him, but, controlling herself, she allowed him to help her down.

So Precious should have departed that next morning, and she would have, too, except that Mannish undertook shuttle diplomacy. He shuttled into the mistress's room and worked his guileful tact, and then he shuttled into Precious's room, sat on the edge of her bed, and begged her to stay. He promised that he would do anything she wanted, anything. He sweet-mouthed her while she lay obdurately on her bed and stared stonily at the ceiling. He reached over and stroked her hair, and then, after pouring honey down her ears for at least a half an hour, he kissed her softly on the lips. She replied with a properly discouraging Christian elbow, but he persisted and was soon kissing neck and caressing bosom and gnawing on her earlobe, suffering full and unmistakable rebuff only when he tried to wriggle tongue down her ear.

"No tongue in earhole, please," she said gruffly enough for him to grasp that he had strayed out of bounds.

After much wooing and cajoling and cuddling with her deep into the night, Mannish perched on a narrow strip on the edge of the bed from which he proceeded to conduct a thoroughly satisfying feel-up of all relevant body parts.

"I am a Christian woman," Precious muttered as a reminder as much to herself as to him, shivering with delight as one particular probe deliciously struck water.

"I know that, Precious," his whisper respectfully assured her. "That is why I intend to use a brand-new condom."

She said, "Oh," the best she could manage on the spur of the moment.

As he mounted her she begged pardon and briefly took time out to turn Theophilus's portrait facedown on the table next to her bed to spare her late husband the distress of witnessing her backsliding carnality when he no doubt already had enough on his mind with learning and rehearsing the angelic hymnal.

"Are you ready, Precious?" Mannish asked huskily, puffing cottonballs softly in the creases of her neck.

Thank you, yes, she was quite ready. Theophilus had been cold now for nearly a year. Burning atop her bosom was a hot-blooded young man, mounted where only emptiness and homesickness had lately ridden.

Her heart was a child with a skip rope.

When Precious awoke the next morning, she drew sweet breath, walked with a sprightly step into the massive double-jointed kitchen. As she warbled through the kitchen preparing breakfast for man and dog, she found herself pausing to stretch and crack her joints of lingering bubbles of sleep, savoring to the full the satisfaction of having reduced a grown man to insensibility against her bosom last night, teaching once again the usual grim lesson about the transitoriness of lust. When she was done with Mannish last night, she was proud to say, not even mythic Beulah herself could have roused a strand of his pubic hair.

She hummed a hymn and mixed a batch of thick waffle batter. Mistress Lucy strolled into the kitchen, accepted a cup of coffee from Precious, and read the newspapers in the strained morning silence that always follows nighttime domestic uproar. Precious thought to mention the row of the night before but decided against it, so other than the obvious burbling about "Morning," neither of them said a word.

Dressed in his uniform, Mannish joined them a half an hour later, his cheeks glowing under a fresh coat of varnish, a schoolboy's glint in his eyes. He sipped a cup of coffee near Precious, who hummed triumphantly under her breath.

Riccardo trotted into the kitchen, heading straight for Precious, when he suddenly stopped, peered suspiciously up at Mannish, and growled.

"What's the matter, sweetheart?" Mistress Lucy crooned.

The dog flicked his glance at her, telegraphed a greeting with a perfunctory wag of his tail, and returned his attention to Mannish with a deeper, angrier growl. Startled, Precious stared down guiltily at him for she knew instinctively what the growl meant. It was a dog reproach for, "Why you give dat Coolie my pum-pum?" asked in such an ill-mannered tone that she felt the rash impulse to bend down and box his face.

"What on earth is wrong with you, Riccardo?" the mistress wondered, reaching down to scoop up her pet. But even settled in her lap, the dog still glared and snarled at Mannish, who feigned indifference.

"Maybe he want a cheese omelet this morning," Precious suggested hopefully.

"Mannish, are you sure you bought unfertilized eggs?" Mistress Lucy worried, massaging Riccardo behind the ears.

"Oh, yes, Miss Johnston," Mannish said suavely. "The hens haven't seen a cock since birth!"

Precious clucked sympathetically and headed for the refrigerator.

Covetous dog eyes tracked her progress.

Chapter 19

"Mummy, how you get yourself in these predicaments, eh?" Shirley asked with that scolding look of perplexity a middle-aged mother dreads to see in a grown daughter. Precious heaved a sigh and twiddled her thumbs with mortification.

It was Sunday, her day off, and Precious was visiting Shirley. The two grandchildren, having just returned from Sunday school, had cavorted off into the nearby woods, seeking respite from biblical morbidness. Henry was pottering in the kitchen, baking a cake, leaving Precious and Shirley briefly alone in the living room, where Precious had just told of her scrapes with the dog.

"I did nothing to encourage dis animal!" Precious declared indignantly.

Shirley got up and paced with official police briskness, dodging between sofa and chair and ending up staring out the window with her back to her mother. She posed briefly there before snapping her fingers with sudden decisiveness.

"I'll run over him for you with my patrol car. I was in hot pursuit. A dog darted into the street, and I ran over him. The suspect escaped. Your troubles are over."

"Murder?" Precious gasped. "You want to murder de dog?"

"Now you talking like an American! You don't *murder* a dog. You run over a dog. Can you let him out tomorrow evening around 8:00? I'll run over him for you then."

Precious gestured irritably. "You take dis for a joke," she grumbled.

"If I miss him with the car, I'll just lean out the window and plug him. You can say that the dog was a victim of drive-by shooting."

Precious shook her head. She would not be a party to murder. If the dog happened to be out in the street for a stroll and Shirley just chanced to come by and felt like running him over on her own accord, that was different.

"You stay there going on fenky-fenky," Shirley declared scornfully, "until the dog hold you down and rape you."

"A dog can't rape a woman, Shirley! Use your brain!"

"A Jamaican dog, maybe. But an American dog damn well can."

"Listen, don't bother with de everlasting American patriotism dis morning! I have enough trouble already."

There was a pause in the conversation while respective digestion of opinion, word, and topic silently took place.

Precious stirred, sighed, and grumbled. "To tell you the truth, I want to go home. It's getting so me nerves can't stand dis place again. I have a headache ever since I come to dis country. Murder, stabbing, shooting morning, noon, and night. Man going berserk in schoolyard and supermarket. Gunman barricading inside house. Woman murdering her husband over a talking parrot. Alien breeding Arizona housewife of two-headed baby. Bigfoot begging bus fare off hikers in Oregon. I can't stand it anymore! I not even eating right. You don't see how I lose weight? Ten pounds, straight off me batty, you father's favorite part. Thank God he's not alive today, he'd go look a young fat gal. Why can't I just dead now and be happy, eh? Instead, Theophilus Higginson, the most miserable man on two foot, get to dead and be safe and happy, while I have to stay here on earth, alive and miserable!"

"Mummy! Leave the fool-fool job. Come back and live with us! You don't need to work."

Shirley's earnest plea was still ringing in the air when Henry sauntered in on the conversation.

"Precious," he asked eagerly, "are you coming back to live with us?"

"Not quite yet," she said dryly.

"Mummy, mind the dog don't hold you down, you know!"

Henry's head swivelled excitably from mother to daughter.

"Dog? What dog? What're you talking about?"

"You wait till I reunite with your father in Paradise, you'll see the good kick I going give him for leaving me in dis predicament."

"Are you guys talking Jamaican dialect?"

"Speaking of Daddy, you never did tell me who Brutus is."

"Mercy!"

"I'm not understanding one word of this conversation, people!"

Days of tension and disagreeable scene followed. The dog began to park himself outside Precious's door every night, whimpering to be let in until Mistress Lucy herself had to come and cart him off to her own boudoir. One morning the mistress opined to Mannish that the dog was such a victim of an insidious *idée fixe* that she wondered whether Precious had put Jamaican voodoo on the poor animal.

"What is the meaning of this *idée fixe*?" Mannish asked with polite bewilderment.

"It means an obsession. Riccardo is obviously obsessed with the Jamaican bitch." She added gloomily, "I blame myself."

"You should not blame yourself, Miss Johnston. The dog is only obeying his karma."

"He got this sick obsessiveness from me. I am the same way. When a man wants me, I kick him. But when a man doesn't want me, I screw him until he does. Then I kick him."

Mannish sniffed with circumspection. "It is a most peculiar contrariness," he said adroitly.

"That's why I'm doomed to one night stands. Once a man finds out that I'm rich, he always begins snivelling. If I could only meet a fabulously rich man who hated me! I'd kiss his ass, give him healthy children, and be happy. If he worked at hating me, the relationship would last forever. Of course, once he had a lapse and started to love me, I'd kick him, and it'd be over."

Mannish scratched his chin and tried to look philosophical.

"So here I am, in my own kitchen," Mistress Lucy added with a shudder of self-abasement, "confiding all this to my Indian chauffeur. No wonder poor Riccardo is so neurotic."

One morning shortly after this heart-to-heart talk between mistress and chauffeur, an ugly scene occurred. Precious was cooking in the kitchen, moaning inwardly about the hardship of boiling soup without a beefy bone. The mistress was at the kitchen table, poring over financial records. Mannish was waxing the Rolls Royce in the courtyard. Riccardo was curled up near Precious's feet, darting lewd glances at her potbellied figure and every now and again wheezing with a lovelorn groan.

"Precious," the mistress said impatiently, "for God's sake, will you please pat Riccardo? Don't you hear him moaning?"

With a forbearing sigh, Precious bent over and briefly dusted the crown of the dog's head, flattening a sprig of fur that sprouted between his sharpened ears. Just then Mannish entered the kitchen. Riccardo growled and jumped up to hover protectively beside Precious.

"It is very hot outside," Mannish declared to the kitchen at large, pouring himself a glass of water.

As if to reply, Riccardo trotted briskly over to the chauffeur and signed his right leg with a flamboyant twirl of piss. Mannish froze. "Riccardo has christened me," he hissed between clenched teeth.

The mistress glanced up with a bemused shaking of her head. "He feels loving today. Must be the heat."

"If I live for ten millennia," Mannish grimaced, "I will know never to steal another man's camels. I have learned my lesson for eternity."

Stalking out of the kitchen, he limped toward his room above the garage.

Mistress Lucy glanced up distractedly. "What was that all about?"

"I don't know, mum." Precious dropped the kitchen towel on the floor, bent over to pick it up, and whispered vehemently at the dog, "Piss 'pon my foot today and is the last foot you piss 'pon on dis earth."

With a nimble thrust of its head, the dog dug deep into her right earhole with its tongue. Precious shrieked and bolted upright as if sprung violently out of a box.

Mistress Lucy looked up peevishly.

"Now what?"

"You cannot butcher and eat the dog, and dat's final. Now stop talking about it."

Precious was in no mood for mincing words. Mannish was brooding in her room, slumped in a chair beside her bed. On a side table lay the butcher knife she had just forcefully extracted from his hand. The mistress had gone to a formal dinner with her date, and three distant hallways away Riccardo was scratching at the door of his bedroom in which Precious had contrived to entrap him. When she had answered the soft knock on her door and found Mannish standing there, Precious naturally assumed that the chauffeur had come to beg her another piece, which she was quite agreeable to giving, provided he was prepared to suffer brief Christian resistance. But instead, she found that he'd come to enlist her help in a harebrained scheme to butcher and cook the dog tonight while the mistress was away.

"I cannot stand it anymore, Precious." The chauffeur slumped in the chair, looking miserable. "I just cannot bear to be pissed on anymore."

"Be a man! Just tell yourself dat you are the one with the soul."

"Yes. You are quite right. I must get ahold of myself." With a disciplined shudder, he seemed to regain his self-control. "So, how are you feeling nowadays?"

Precious shrugged to indicate eternal bowing to God's will. "Nearly five thousand in the bank. Black market rate is now fifty-nine dollars with hopes for sixty dollars to one coming up. I soon go home now."

Mannish leaned over her chair and kissed her tenderly. "I am praying for a fall in this black market rate. I will miss you very much."

After he had spent an hour of sincere, respectable begging, Precious's conscience was clear enough to permit dignified removal of her panties.

A few moments later, as they were passionately entwined abed, the dog erupted in a hellish, amplified howling that pulsated in ghoulish waves down the darkened hallways.

"It is the hound of the Baskervilles," Mannish stopped to mutter darkly.

"Forget the dog, man!" Precious panted urgently.

"Sorry."

Mannish returned stoutly to his labors, but he soon faltered; so unnerved was he by the unremitting howling that within seconds he was wriggling atop her slippery and naked like a stranded eel.

"Precious," he groaned, "I am so sorry. I can think of nothing but this ghastly howling."

Precious sighed. With encouraging words and pats, she slid the wilted chauffeur off her bosom and ushered him under cover of face-saving darkness to her bedroom door. Pausing in the open doorway, they could hear salvos of beastly howls whistling down the dim hallways and splattering in the empty living room. Mannish was so self-reproachful and nervous that he hadn't even dressed, and it was all Precious could do to calm his apologetic babbling and send him trudging down the hall, forlornly dragging after him a useless pair of crumpled pants. She watched until the wiggle of his brown batty had been blotted up by the household dimness before quietly closing her door.

Yet another grisly scene ensued.

The mistress was away again, this time at a day-long meeting, and Precious was slaving in the kitchen over a vegetarian stew. His amatory lapse already a week old, Mannish still slunk discreetly out of reach whenever she approached, and although Precious felt sorry for him and tried hard to think of a biblical parable to cheer him up, she finally decided that scripture should not be quoted to console fainthearted hood. Moreover, the dog was playing her watchman with unusual vigilance, and the chauffeur had only to walk into a room in which she was present to convulse the beast into a fit of snarling.

This afternoon, Precious was warbling a hymn and feeling fairly content with life as she stirred the stew and bustled about the spacious kitchen, Riccardo padding in her wake. She sat down briefly at the kitchen table and the dog was instantly at her side, peering at her with watery eyes and trying to vacuum vapors from her crotch with its nasty nose.

Mannish came into the kitchen, looking for a rag. With a snarl, Riccardo darted over to him, closing fast at an unmistakable christening angle.

"No!" Mannish barked, scooting around the kitchen table at which Precious sat. "Precious," he pleaded, "he wants to christen me again!"

"Leave the man pants foot alone, dog!" Precious commanded, bending over to swat halfheartedly at the animal. Riccardo dodged her swipe and drove pell-mell for the chauffeur.

Around the table whirled two blurry figures, Precious's head serving as their makeshift maypole.

"Stop it!" she yelled, getting dizzy and nearly losing her balance and toppling off the chair.

"I have already been christened!" Mannish bawled.

With a nimble jump, he hurdled a chair, threw open the back door, and galloped into the courtyard, the dog plunging after him. Precious stumbled in pursuit, yelling for Riccardo to stop.

In the backyard, after a breathless run, she found Mannish perched atop the low-lying branch of a tree, with Riccardo agitatedly circling its trunk, yapping shrilly.

The chauffeur went berserk. Laughing maniacally, he unzipped his fly and aimed a malicious arc of human piss at the circling dog. Precious shrieked at the unpleasant sight of a urinating hood, something she had not glimpsed since girlhood, and shielded her eyes. The dog scurried away from the drizzle with a dissenting yip.

"Stop you wee-weeing on the dog!" Precious bellowed, her eyes closed. "Who going wash him now dat you wet him up? Stop it!"

Order was restored by her bellowing. When she opened her eyes again, hood was thankfully out of sight, but Mannish still sulked on the branch.

"I'm sorry, Precious. He has driven me temporarily mad."

"Dis is not how you behave in a mansion!" she shrieked with frustration.

Riccardo nuzzled up to her foot as if to agree, directing a scolding snarl at the treed chauffeur.

"Now I going have to bathe you wee-wee off de brute!" she groused, coaxing the dog into the house for a wash.

After she had bathed the dog, Precious returned to the backyard to find Mannish sullenly slouching behind the tree. He mumbled another round of apologies, and Precious told him she had not come to listen to his excuses for infantile behavior, but to convince him to allow the dog to christen him in peace here and now, or there was bound to be dickens to pay later when the mistress came home.

Mannish scuffed at the brick paving with an aggrieved shoe.

"You are getting too Americanized," he remarked petulantly.

Precious heatedly denied that she was becoming Americanized. But she had studied the dog brain and knew that once he had made up his mind to christen a foot, he would christen the foot, and it was better to caulk up you eye and let the dog have free with you foot now while the mistress was away than wait until the mistress came back when he would have free with you foot anyway and you might kick him and lose you work.

"All right!" Mannish snapped in the face of unassailable logic. "Bring on the stinking beast. Let my foot be his urinal!"

Precious nodded, went into the house to fetch him, and returned with Riccardo trotting at her side.

The dog immediately bounded over to the sitting-duck chauffeur, circled briefly to establish the range, then brusquely lifted its leg and performed the nastiness.

"Is he finished?" Mannish asked through closed eyes and clenched teeth.

"All done," Precious sang.

The chauffeur opened his eyes, shook off his pants leg, and marched grimly toward his room above the garage.

He turned to hiss murderously, "One day, I am going to cook and eat that dog. America will not turn me into a fire hydrant without a fight."

Chapter 20

As an old time housewife Precious grimly knew that hood was only an earthbound ornament which man shed immediately upon assuming a spiritual form after death, hood and batty being two bodily parts definitely not retained in the resurrection. That argument, of course, had had absolutely no influence on the living Theophilus, for when he would frequently come panting after her during the hotblooded days of his youth to remind him that his wayward hood would never see inside the gates of heaven only made him furious. He would snarl irritably, "Listen, woman! Don't chat no rubbish in me ear!"

So in her own way Precious knew how to cope with a slack man. But she did not know how to cope with the attentions of Riccardo, and the only frail blessing she could see in this nasty dog wooing was that it was happening to her in a foreign land.

Indeed, if this had happened to her in Jamaica, the backyard gossiping would already be raging. A few understanding souls would absolve Precious and blame the dog, complaining that in Jamaica today a woman couldn't even go about her business without dog hood popping up in her path while the good-for-nothing government did nothing. But other tongues would maliciously lash at poor Precious's reputation and accuse her of leading the dog on, with some backbiting sisters sarcastically asking stupefied husbands questions that man mouth would never dare answer, such as, "She say a dog try grind her . . . How come no dog ever tried to grind me? What happen? Don't my batty fat, too?"

In the mansion tension was building, and plotting was going on, and subterfuge and ruse were being waged as Precious tried her best to dampen the ardor of the dog, to keep him at foot's length, to discourage his amorousness. And the mistress continued to think the beastly business funny. She laughed her head off in the kitchen when the dog would occasionally lock its forelegs around Precious's foot and squeegee its sticky hood up and down her shinbone.

Precious would shriek, "Dog grinding me foot!" and shake off the beast and dash into another room, and the mistress would howl with glee and pass some snide remark like, "Precious, Riccardo just loves you!" From behind the door Precious would shriek what went without saying in any other country but this mad America, "I am a decent woman! I am a Christian! De dog is out of order to grind me foot!" To which the mistress would cynically reply, "We all come from the same stone, Precious! Stop being so ridiculously speciest!"

None of this Precious understood. She did not understand how dog could come from stone, to say nothing of a river-baptized sister, and if she had understood the reference, she would have hotly argued that common ancestry still gave the dog no right to grind her. She just knew that she couldn't stay any longer in the mansion with the dog mewling lewdly beneath her tailbone.

She made up her mind to give notice and return to Jamaica. Enough was enough. She was finished, through; she was done with the out of order dog, mansion, and America.

The next evening she told Mannish she was finished. The mistress and the dog were spending the night away. Mannish had dropped them off and returned to the mansion, and now he and Precious lolled in the living room and cocked up foot as if they were the rightful owners of all the lavish surrounding wealth.

She could not go on, Precious blurted out bluntly. She had gotten to the point where she was ashamed even to go to church, where hymns choked in her gullet, where knee would not freely bend in lawful worship. Although her conscience was clear that she had done nothing to encourage the nasty animal, if she allowed matters to carry on this way people would talk.

The chauffeur looked wistful and begged her not to leave. He had been drinking wine, which made his ripened face sag like a flaccid balloon, and he tried to make light of her trouble by remarking, "You have the same effect on me as on this dog."

"You think dis is a joke? You think dat my foot is a dog grinding post? You think I migrate to America to become a laughing stock?"

Mannish said he thought no such thing, that he respected her and admired her sense of dignity and deportment and was begging her not to go.

"How can a woman have dignity and deportment when every time she look behind her she see a dog hood longing out for her?" Precious wanted to know, eyes blazing.

Mannish finally admitted that he did not know. He sipped the wine and thought about it, wearing the faraway and perplexed look of a child puzzling over some nursery rhyme story such as why a thiefing brute like that good-for-nothing high-school dropout Jack should be allowed to scale a beanstalk, thief a householder's personal possessions and poultry, murder the man when he gave pursuit, and live happily ever after off his ill-gotten gains without getting the gallows. Then he brightened and snapped up erect in his chair.

"I have it, Precious," he said briskly. "I have the solution. I will purchase a bitch in heat for Riccardo. The mistress will not know, for I will keep the bitch at my cousin's house. When Riccardo becomes amorous, we will bring her to him."

"But isn't dat what I heard a television preacher call 'wanton recreational sex?'" Precious fretted.

"It is moral and purposeful sex! It will make everyone happy. It is the perfect solution!"

Precious was uncertain that that was the solution but she could think of no other objection except her nagging doubts about introducing recreational sex into the animal kingdom. She said that she wished he would do something, anything, just to give her an ease from the pushy dog. Mannish got up and came over to where she was sitting. He bent down and kissed her warmly.

"Precious," he said huskily, nuzzling her neck, "I know that since my Babylonian days my outlook has been indecisive, but I promise you that I will do this thing for you."

He said other things, mainly clumps of sugary endearments, and tried to perch her palm atop his stiff hood as if a woman's hand had been specially created to perform such untoward capping. Precious, however, pulled her hand away, mumbling that in her present confused frame of mind the sight or touch of any hood would only remind her of the dog. So he kissed her and hugged her and nuzzled her and begged her to at least administer a light brushing of his pant-front steeple for encouragement, but Precious stoutly refused.

The next morning Mannish tried to find a bitch in heat for Riccardo.

* * *

The first ASPCA office he called hotly informed him that because pound animals are fixed, they were never in heat. Moreover, the woman on the other end of the line asked just what he intended to do with a bitch in heat, implying that she suspected bestiality. Mannish stiffly retorted that the bitch was not for him, but for his bulldog. There was a stunned silence at the other end of the line before the woman informed him that the American Society for the Prevention of Cruelty to Animals was not a whorehouse.

Mannish hung up. "Stupid woman," he muttered.

He dialed another pound and the conversation went much the same way and had the same outcome.

"Hello," Mannish began brightly, "I'm calling to ask if you have female dogs suitable for adoption."

"Certainly, sir. We have many different kinds of dogs here."

"Would you happen to have a bitch who is in heat?"

There was a sudden pause; the telephone wire hissed.

"In heat? You want a bitch in heat? Why?"

"She is for my bulldog. He is feeling frisky."

"Sir, our animals are not for surrogate sex."

"I just thought that you might have one bitch in heat who has not yet been neutered."

Another menacing pause.

"Sir, what is your accent? Are you from Vietnam?"

"Certainly not!"

"May I have your name and address please?"

Mannish hung up quickly.

He had similar rebuffs calling up want ads advertising dogs for sale. One indignant man on the other end of the line said that he was prepared to shoot any foreigner who tried to buy one of his dogs and turn her into a slut and who the hell did he think he was coming here from overseas to whore American dogs?

"Come over and be shot, Saddam Hussein," the man nastily invited.

Mannish asked the man if he didn't think that dogs screwed, too, and why was he making such a fuss about such a harmless request.

"Dogs screw, too? That's how you foreign bastards think, eh? What'd you do, you bastard, beat the poor animals until they give you a filthy peep show?"

"It's no use," Mannish mumbled to Precious that evening. "There are no bitches in heat in America. And if there are, you cannot buy one. The only suggestion I have is that we drive around and try to locate one for dognapping on the street."

Precious sniffed and asked one picky question. "Who, pray, going get out of the Rolls Royce and stoop down on the sidewalk pavement to look up dog batty and see if de bitch in heat?"

"I will be doing the driving, Precious," Mannish mumbled defensively. "Riccardo is not after me."

"I am not looking up no dog batty on de street corner, Mister Mannish Chaudhuri! I am a forty-eight-year-old Christian grandmother!"

Chapter 21

The next day the dog came down with an ear infection. Precious had been indignantly wondering when creation would take righteous retribution against the lecherous mongrel, so she blurted out a jubilant "Hallelujah!" at this infestation of heaven-sent ear bacteria and chortled another triumphant cry when the veterinarian's medication reduced the beast to a zombie, making him too weak to even grind a big toe.

So she had a few days of peace and quiet when no dog padded under the overhang of her batty or tried to copulate with her shinbone, and she was free to make leisurely plans for returning to Jamaica.

On the third morning she was feeling such unaccustomed contentment that when she made her way early into the kitchen she was humming a hymn and didn't even notice the mistress clad in a hairy coat and installed in her customary place at the breakfast table with Riccardo curled up at her feet. Nor did she spot the reckless glint that lighted up in the mistress's eyes at her approach.

Precious was running water for breakfast tea before she became aware of the mistress. She started and murmured apologetically, "Morning, mum. Nice coat."

"It's a mink," the mistress snapped impatiently.

Precious said that she never knew and muttered something to the effect that before she had her morning tea she couldn't tell mink from mango, for her eyes did not adjust to morning light as well as they used to before her senses had become bogged down in middle age.

"Precious, I am wearing an animal pelt!" the mistress cried, stamping her foot.

Precious heaved a sigh and puzzled about what she was expected to say, when Mannish blustered into the kitchen, glanced at the mink, and gasped that he felt faint. Reeling dizzily, he grabbed for the nearest neckback, which belonged to Precious, nearly toppling her onto the floor.

Precious shrieked and clutched at the kitchen counter to steady herself, while Riccardo brayed a sickly growl and staggered up before imploding in a pile of dog joint and fur on the kitchen floor.

Mistress Lucy beamed at the excitement.

What they were witnessing, Mistress Lucy declared as she sashayed around the kitchen like the Queen of Sheba, was the only moral mink coat in the world. Here she paused, giving Mannish the opportunity to express his shock by shamming hyperventilation.

Every animal from which the coat had been made, continued the mistress, had been hand-butchered by God.

Precious squawked, "God is nobody's butcher, Mistress Lucy! Burn me to de stake, but I still maintain as much."

Mistress Lucy said nobody was going to burn anybody to the stake this morning, thank you. The phrase only meant that no pelt in the coat had been removed until the mink had suffered freely visited organic death. And before the pelt was removed, an autopsy was conducted to determine that the animal had been felled by such God-given disease as wholesome heart attack or natural stroke. The coat came with miniaturized death certificates signed by a veterinarian certifying that it was made of one hundred percent organic-death pelts, all profits being recycled to provide an Edenic environment for future mink generations. What could be more humane? And with God being the sole butcher . . .

"Mistress Lucy!" Precious protested. "Almighty God is no butcher!"

"So if man isn't killing the mink, who is?" Mistress Lucy asked, toying with her maid.

"Nature, mum."

"And who do Christians say made nature?"

"De devil, mum. De coat is a demon coat."

The mistress glared at Precious with contempt and ordered Mannish to call and arrange for her jet plane to be ready to leave that morning. She was personally going to tour this break-through mink farm in North Dakota and see for herself how it was managed, for it was simply too utopian to be believed. If she liked what she saw, she intended to buy it.

With that she scooped up Riccardo and stalked out of the kitchen.

Mannish exhaled wearily. "Precious, why must you always crush another soul's happiness?"

"What a way you catch you breath all of a sudden!" Precious rejoined sarcastically.

"I must have a place to live while I am awaiting Beulah," Mannish mumbled apologetically. "It will not be easy for me later, atoning for the stolen camels."

"Praise God I soon depart from dis madhouse!"

So the mistress went away to North Dakota, leaving behind an ailing Riccardo even though Precious tried to inveigle her into taking the dog along on the trip. But the mistress said no, she did not want to take a chance on hurting Riccardo, whom she kissed full on the mouth before she flounced out of the room bawling for Mannish to come and carry her luggage. Then she was gone and Precious was left ogling the dog sprawled on his mistress's bed.

"You better not trouble me while de mistress is away," Precious warned the animal, aiming a stern finger at his head.

The dog stirred, looked up at her with rheumy eyes, and blew bad breath all over her finger.

And things went well that first day, for Riccardo was still groggy from the medicine. Precious ushered him through a halfhearted turn around his favorite hydrants and fed him an early supper. Then she turned down his capacious bed and the dog jumped onto it, curled up in its middle, and fell quickly asleep.

But by two days later, the dog had become frisky again. Twice on the second day of the mistress's absence he treed Precious on the breakfast table with his aggressive wooing.

The mistress called repeatedly, inquiring if Riccardo was well, and one time Precious had to bring the dog to the telephone so the mistress could coax him into giving her a bedtime bark.

After that telephone call, Precious managed to entice the dog into his bedroom early in the evening and hurriedly slam the door on him, causing the brute to begin an impassioned howling that jangled her nerves and made her hands shake. Mannish suggested that they go out in the Rolls Royce and have dinner, leaving the beast to howl himself to death.

They had wine. They shared deep talk. They chatted about the mistress and her eccentric ways. They drove home languidly in the Rolls Royce. And when they got back to the darkened mansion they heard howls still bellowing in the mansion's darkened rooms, rattling throughout the emptiness of the house with a ghoulish hollowness. It would be impossible for her to sleep with such a racket, Mannish said, she should come and stay in his quarters above the garage, where no dog howling could reach her ears.

Precious was reluctant at first, for she did not wish to pass the whole night with a man to whom she was not married, but eventually the dog howling upset her nerves so much that she followed the chauffeur into his quarters, where he promptly began to beg her a grind.

She hesitated, confessing that she was getting tired of giving grind to a sinner. It would be all right if she felt that he had prospects of salvation, but she thought it improper to be constantly giving grind to a man who had never been baptized. Mannish swore fervently that he was prepared to repent and convert on the spot. Precious said that he shouldn't make a joke of it because that would only make the fire hotter, but Mannish assured her that he was not joking.

One thing led to another, and after Mannish had endured some more chastening talk about his disbelieving ways, he ended up naked atop her belly. Once he had settled there she promptly forgot religion and set about the worldly task of reducing him to the usual dribbling nub. He fell asleep at her side, his lips nibbling idly on her right nipple.

She was going to box him for this, but she held her hand. It was needless, this nibbling, which to Precious's thinking meant that it was most likely a sin. A pre-grind nibble was workmanlike and necessary; but a post-grind nibble was a hoggish wallowing. However, for the time being, since Mannish was still unsaved, she would permit him to nibble sleepily at her nipple, thinking with a grim sniff that he had better enjoy it now because his nibbling days were numbered.

She had had a change of heart and had decided that she would not quit the mansion. She would remain and suffer lewd dog courtship for the sake of her lover. Under her watchful eye Mannish would be born again, and she would personally save his soul. There would be no backsliding, either, for once she saved a soul it stayed saved.

She was dreamily thinking of the regimen she intended to put him under when she fell asleep.

Sometime later that night Precious awoke on Mannish's bed to the noise of an unearthly snoring that her ears could not believe blew out the small nosehole of a Coolie. It sounded like two baby mules were stuffed up his nostrils with each trying to out-snort the other, using nosehole as a makeshift echo chamber. She elbowed Mannish onto his side and the left mule stopped its snoring while the right one sounded an ugly bray of undeserved victory.

Precious raised herself on her elbow to look out the open window above the bed at a clear and cloudless night sky with metallic yellow light purling through the crescent slit of a new moon. The air was brisk and sweet with nighttime scents and starlight sparkle, and through the window she could see the darkened sweep and breadth of the mansion's gardens shimmering in the night breeze. She could not sleep beside a man who made such atrocious noises, so she fumbled with a sigh for her clothes that he had considerately removed and neatly folded in a tidy cocoon at the foot of the bed.

Frock was there, wrapped protectively around slip and brassiere. Burrowed deep inside the pile were her fallen panties. She stood up beside the bed, intending to dress, and glanced curiously at the night sky.

That was when an idea stunned her: Why bother dress?

Precious had been living in a mansion now for nearly a year and had yet to walk naked among its arrayed splendors. She had not walked naked through the front yard, the backyard, the side yard with its ornamental rose gardens and flagstone paths. She had never walked naked through the corpulently furnished living room, the sinewy picture-lined hallways, the dining room crammed with the formal props and implements of decorative gluttony.

Now it was true, and Precious grasped this immediately, that no one in Jamaica upon learning of her life in an American mansion would ever pass a catty remark about her fainthearted failure to walk naked through a mansion's drawing room when she had had the chance. And it was also true that she herself would never boast even to relatives that hers was the only batty in the family to have ever strolled bare through a mansion.

Yet the idea of standing, of walking, or perhaps even performing a languid ballerina pirouette naked inside a mansion was one she found so utterly exciting that it made her shiver.

Years later, when she looked back on this moment, Precious would wonder how a woman of her upbringing could have fallen prey to such a depraved thought, and the only sensible explanation she could give was that the human heart was a cave hung with dark, upside-down impulses. One had taken wing and flown into her brain while her senses were still under the spell of that false prophet, hood.

Before her better nature could take arms against this impure whim, she had collected her clothes, tiptoed through the dark room, and stepped ecstatically out the door and into the nighttime coolness.

She stood naked on the top of the stairs, drew an exhilarating breath, and surveyed the darkened land shimmering under the

waxy light dripping from the chinky new moon. The nighttime
air trickled over her batty and poured a moist coolness into
every body crack. Darkness daubed damply at her breasts, and
the moment held a raw deliciousness that made her tingle.

Carefully, looking warily at every step, she made her way
down the stairs and padded across the brick surface of the
backyard and into the house.

She entered through the kitchen door, closed it softly
behind her with a furtive click, and poised there swaddled in
the household shadows.

One deep cleansing breath, and she had ghosted into the
drawing room, and slowly, majestically—or so she fantasized—
was executing a pirouette of triumph beside an ornate coffee
table when suddenly a stumpy shadow lurched out from under
the banquet table and a tongue stabbed deep into her batty
crack, greasing it with oily mouthwater.

Precious shrieked, for she had a delirious sense that the
coffee table had slimed her with a netherworld nighttime
tongue. She jumped backwards in the darkness with a second
cry of horror answered by an implacable growl and the fierce
grip of her legs between hairy tentacles.

"Riccardo!" Precious screamed, dimly understanding. "Stop
it! How you get out? Leggo me foot!"

She bolted down the hallway, tripped on the edge of an
Oriental rug, and sprawled facedown on the floor. With a
frenzied growl, the dog sprang atop her fleshy buttocks and
began pumping, and she felt some hideously slimy puncheon
ice-picking dimples into her batty cheeks. She rolled over on
her back, flailing with her arms and legs at the thrusting,
probing, licking animal whose turgid belly drummed with a
ravenous growling.

"Help! Murder! Police!" Precious bawled. "Dog grind!"

Screaming, she wedged her leg under the pulsating underbelly of the snarling beast and, giving a mighty heave, shot him spinning toward the ceiling as from a catapult.

She did not hear him fall or thud, but suddenly the room pulsed with only the rasp of her own convulsed wheezing.

She scrambled to her feet and fled down the hall. Then she stopped to breathlessly listen, darted down the hallway through the elegant drawing room, and sprinted out into the backyard and up the stairs above the garage.

She scrambled to Mannish's bedside, hysterically slapping at the chauffeur and shaking him awake.

Mannish sat up groggily, while she babbled incoherently about "attempted dog grind." He tumbled after her down the rattling stairs and into the living room, which he blasted with a garish overhead light and, while Precious shielded her eyes and blubbered at him to protect her from dog rape, stalked cautiously over to a far corner of the room.

He strolled calmly to her side. "Precious," he exploded in a gleeful laugh. "The beast is dead! Thanks be to Krishna!"

He added the observation, almost as a polite filler in the stunned silence, "Precious, you are naked."

"Is *you* take off me clothes!" she shrieked, desperate to implicate another culprit in her crime. "Is *you* peel off every stitch of clothing off me body!"

She was cowering in a corner, her hands trembling uncontrollably, her eyes owlishly gaping.

"Lawd!" she screeched hysterically, indignantly, "you drop de tin can 'pon me head again!"

Chapter 22

Precious hurried back to Jamaica that very day. She departed in a fit of hysterics, trailing behind her an unremitting flow of babbled explanations and justifications which Mannish assured her were unnecessary, for he thought it quite splendid that she had killed the stinking dog and if she would only not be hasty he was sure he could concoct some explanation of the dog's demise to satisfy the mistress. But Precious panicked, convinced that once the mistress discovered her dog was dead she would run right out and book a freelance gunman to kill her Jamaican maid. She begged the chauffeur to say how long he thought it would take the mistress to hire a murderer through a magazine advertisement as she had seen on a television show. Mannish denied that the mistress would ever do such a thing, but in the face of persistent grilling and hysterical pleading, he grudgingly estimated that it would take at least two weeks. The mistress might be rich, but she drove a hard bargain and would need at least a fortnight to haggle down the fee of any gunmen who responded to her advertisements.

"You take dis for a joke, Mannish Chaudhuri!" Precious shrieked. "It is not a joke! It was an accident!"

"Precious, it was a godsend. I beg you not to leave!"

But Precious would not stay. She would not be reasoned with. And she would not be mollified by schemes to dupe the mistress about what had really happened, by farfetched explanations Mannish was cooking up to explain the death of the dog. He was never specific with her when she demanded to know what earthly explanation of the dog's death he was so sure would satisfy the mistress, but he kept insisting, "Precious, it will be all right. Leave the mistress to me."

"I don't want my bullet-riddled carcass displayed on de 6 o'clock news and used to sell toilet paper," she ranted.

"Your carcass will not be displayed, Precious. This hatred of publicity is affecting your rationality."

She crammed all her earthly belongings into the two battered suitcases she had brought with her from Jamaica and took a quick bath so she would at least return to her homeland smelling fresh and clean. Then she phoned Shirley to explain what had happened.

Shirley also implored her not to bolt to Jamaica, saying that she could come back to her house in Miami and stay there with no fear whatsoever of local gunman.

"Mummy," she pleaded, "profit from your experience. Dis could be de start of a whole new career for you!"

How could a decent woman profit from fending off the unwanted attentions of an animal? What kind of career was she talking about? Precious demanded.

Shirley babbled desperately: It was about time someone came forward and boldly told the truth about horny Rover and Fido. How many millions of American women were at this moment silently suffering the heartbreak of domestic dog rape? Precious could become a nationally recognized lecturer on DRS, dog rape syndrome. She might sell her story to a tabloid. Who could say where such publicity could lead? Appearances on talk shows? A made-for-television movie?

Precious interrupted wearily.

"Kiss de children for me. I make up my mind. I will write you. I'm leaving before Mistress Lucy come back and find her dog dead."

Mannish waved frenziedly at her when he heard her say this and piped from across the room, "The dog will not be dead here when the mistress returns! I want him as a souvenir."

Precious hung up and angrily confronted the chauffeur. "I did not kill dat dog so dat you can turn him into a souvenir! How much more bizarre and mad can de world turn all of a sudden?"

"I'm sorry, Precious. If you want to take the dog, of course, you are entitled to him."

"I don't want de dog! De dog is dead! Nobody in dis country understands me! Least of all you!"

"Then if you don't want him, why cannot I have him?"

"For what? To eat?"

"I will give him to my cousin to freeze-dry."

Precious shrugged an ignominious surrender, for it was plainly no use. She couldn't cope. Nothing made any sense anymore. In her mind, the world had torn loose from its mooring and wobbled in inky space beyond prophecy. There was no path, no light, no edging darkness to guide the foot of the uncertain pilgrim. She muttered that he could do what he wanted, so long as he took her to the airport, and with this pronouncement she collapsed into a chair.

He helped her lug the suitcases into the trunk of the Rolls Royce, and just before they left, he wrapped the late would-be rapist in a carpet and stuffed him in the trunk.

"You pack dat animal next to me luggage?" Precious carped.

"He is securely wrapped. He is not touching your luggage."

Nevertheless, as they departed for the airport she still grumbled that there would be trouble if she found dog corpse rubbing up against her two grips.

On their way to the airport they stopped at the freeze-drying establishment of the cousin, a laughing relative much like an uncle from Precious's youth who took the whole world as a big joke. The cousin cackled with laughter when they entered, and gave off much the same cackle when Mannish unwrapped the dog from the carpet and asked that he be mummified in the freeze-drying chamber.

"How did the dog die?" wondered the cousin, filling out an official-looking form. With Precious grimly present, Mannish delicately said that it was a long story, and this cryptic utterance caused another stringy cackle to wriggle out of the cousin's mouth.

They were standing in a whitewashed room that looked as if its walls had been repeatedly hand-scrubbed. The air smelled acridly of antiseptic like a hospital's toilet. Before them was a metallic door posted with a sign that said, *Do Not Enter*. Crouched at the entrance to the dingy room, which served both as the cousin's reception area and personal office, was a dog coiled to spring friskily up at visitors. Precious had shied away from him when she first timidly followed Mannish into the room, but the cousin assured her that it was only a display to show off the results of the freeze-drying chamber, which was vastly superior to taxidermy. He was very proud of his machine, purred the laughing cousin, inviting Precious to stroke the dog's head and see if she could tell death with her touch. Precious shuddered and declined.

"I am now very curious," pressed the cousin. "How did this animal die?"

This was to be her punishment, her burden, her personal cross; Precious made up her mind that she would shoulder it uncomplainingly and not put aside the bitter cup.

"He tried to rape me," she said with statuesque dignity. "I threw him off. He hit his head. It was an accident."

The cousin exploded in a burst of laughter and spittle.

The American continent was slipping past the Rolls Royce as they continued their drive to the airport, with Precious gazing wistfully out the window. She was feeling bitterness and spite toward everything American, and if she had had a flag and a match, she would definitely have started a constitutional fire.

"Precious," Mannish softly interrupted her reverie, "would you like to stop here for breakfast?"

She nodded sullen assent. The Rolls Royce, substantial and smooth as a rolling house, purred into the driveway of a McDonald's and pulled up incongruously next to a battered pickup truck plastered over with bumper-sticker American flags.

"I wonder what dis patriot would have to say about what dat American dog try to do to me?" Precious asked bitterly as they stepped out of the Rolls.

"I would not ask questions of American patriots, Precious," Mannish advised softly, holding the car door open for her. "Their abstractness of thought makes them dangerous. They are likely to shoot at querulous immigrants."

They had a glum breakfast. Precious picked at her food with no appetite and sighed frequently as she glanced around the crowded dining room.

"Now I know how a man feels when he is wrongly hanged," she muttered.

Mannish shook his head sympathetically and chewed with feeling on his sausage biscuit. He had never been hanged in his earlier lives, he declared, although once he came so close that the noose was around his neck before the unfortunate mistake was discovered.

"Up to last night," Precious muttered, "I felt like the world was sane."

"The feeling will return shortly, Precious. I am confident."

"I hope you right. I'm only forty-eight. Living in a world I thought was mad could drive me mad."

They finished breakfast on this uneasy note and headed for the car.

Bustling through the front door as they exited the restaurant was a brisk young woman clad in the rind of a snugly tailored business suit. Mannish held open the door for her with a deferential smile.

"You don't have to hold a door open for me," she snapped. "I have a hand of my own. After you."

Mannish was in the parking lot when he staggered, whirled, and gaped after the woman. "It's Beulah!" he gasped.

"It is not!"

"Precious! It is her! Oh, if she ever heard such grammar. I mean, it is she. Wait here!"

"Come back here at once!" yelped Precious, but the chauffeur had already darted back into the restaurant and disappeared.

Precious stood melting in the warming sun before she made a moan of despair and went back inside to search for the chauffeur. She spotted him standing beside a table in a corner engaged in earnest conversation with the woman, who was staring at him suspiciously.

Precious tramped over and parked her bulk conspicuously near his elbow.

"Before I call the police on your friend," the woman asked her crossly, "tell me, how did he know that my name is Beulah?"

Chapter 23

Precious ended up taking a cab to the airport and boarding the plane with not even a life insurance salesman to wave her goodbye. She sat at a window seat and as the aircraft began to rumble down the runway, she silently begged it to crash. It did not comply but lifted off and roared into the heavens, retracting its wheels with a bone-jarring crunch that trickled through the flooring.

She glanced around the crowded aircraft, took in the usual motley collection of women and children, and withdrew her wish for a crash as selfish. But then she remembered reading about a woman in an airplane whose window had exploded, sucking her and her alone out into the sky to splatter 35,000 feet below on a farmer's soybean field, and she asked for this to be her fate. She was right by the window and could be siphoned out without taking any unwilling passengers along. But the aircraft held intact; the window refused to shatter, and the flight was depressingly boring.

Over Cuba a nervous higgler sitting beside her mumbled that she always had nightmares about crashing on Cuban soil and being forced to learn Spanish, a foreign tongue she detested. Precious assured her that she had nothing to fear, for this was an unreliable, headstrong world that did exactly what it wanted to do for its own petty pleasure. It was very much like this airline, she added, which if it ever crashed you could be sure would crash only when it pleased. The higgler looked uneasy and mumbled that she had never heard anyone talk about the world or an airline in such a way but that it was true, the world was really devilishly perverse. Then remembering that she was not on the earth but perched 35,000 feet above it, the higgler lapsed into a nervous and morose silence during which she fidgeted with the airsickness bag and flicked apprehensive glances around the cabin.

Beside her sat Precious with her eyes closed, intermittently requesting a crash, a sucking-out of the window, and assorted other calamities—she would even have settled for a heart attack—but as per usual life merrily bubbled inside her and the plane landed with a willful, provoking smoothness.

When Harold shook himself loose from the swirling crowd and elbowed a path across the pavement to greet her outside the airport, Precious had one flat answer to give to his babbling questions about why she had so abruptly returned from America: "Harold, I am a changed woman."

Precious was a changed woman. She had no fear. She knew no anxiety. She suffered no dread. She did not know why she felt as she did, but she was a woman definitely changed enough to be styled eccentric or, at best, new. Harold chose to say "new" because Precious was his mother and he couldn't bear to think that the belly out of which he had squirted onto this earth had grown eccentric. Mildred chose to say "eccentric," arming herself with that damning wifely comment, "You mad just like you mother!" for use in future marital spats.

Precious was so new that she stayed with Harold for only two nights before she began clamoring to go back to her house in the mountains. Harold protested that she could not stay up there all alone, but Precious insisted that that was just what she wanted to do, and she was backed quickly by Mildred, who argued that a woman could do exactly what she wanted to do, this being modern Jamaica and not your slavery days, and if a mother-in-law wanted to move out of her adult son's house where she was always welcome but definitely didn't belong, she was entitled to do so without opposition.

Harold gave in with a tired sigh.

The next day he drove Precious back to her house in the mountains where he insisted on staying with her that first night, but Precious showed him the shotgun in the closet and the two big dogs, one of which lunged at his ankle, and sweetly reminded him that she was the said woman who had once wiped his batty.

"Look at dis place, Mummy," Harold pleaded, his hand brushing at the crumpled mountains like a disgruntled storekeeper gesturing at unsold goods.

"Kiss me," Precious ordered, presenting a chubby cheek. "Then go home to you wife and family."

As soon as her son had grudgingly driven away, Precious tromped into her bedroom and slid on the cold wooden floor under the bed.

"I know you must be under here!" she called to Jamaican Jesus in a voice so loud that it made the dogs stir on the veranda. "Things need explaining!"

She waited for the explanation.

Chapter 24

She got no explanation, of course, for Massah God does not have to explain His ways to creatures who amble over His earth, whether they walk on foot, fly through air, swim in water, squirm through mud, hang from tree limb, or crawl on dirt. He did not explain to Job and He certainly wouldn't stoop to explain to a disgruntled country widow who dared criticize the Divine Plan. As Precious was not even a lance corporal in the army of righteousness, it was most out of order for her to batter down the tent flap of the commanding general and demand strategic explanation.

All this and more was counselled to Precious by the pastor of her church, who had himself become a widower while Precious was in America and to whom the story of her migration adventures was gradually revealed over the course of the following months. The tale about the attempted dog rape came out one night on her veranda after the pastor impudently christened Precious the juiciest sister in his congregation. At this comment, Precious had very nearly run him off her mountaintop. She blasted him in no uncertain terms that he was out of order to come call her juicy on her own veranda. He apologized and said that he meant no disrespect, adding sulkily that most women would love to hear that a man thought them juicy.

"So what if a dog think me juicy, too?" Precious raged. "What I supposed to do with dat?"

The parson was stunned. He could not comprehend how a dog dared think a Christian woman juicy and said so bluntly.

With this opening, the story of Precious and the unruly American dog, couched in half-truths and euphemisms, wriggled out bashfully on the veranda like mortal sin in a cramped confessional. Naturally, one or two small details—her intimacy with Mannish for one, her naked parading through the mansion for another—remained unrevealed.

Once he had a semblance of the whole story, the parson sat erect in his chair and addressed himself to the faultfinding query implicit in it: how such a scandal could have befallen a decent, well-groomed sister. The answer was, he declaimed in a tone better suited to a pulpit than a quiet veranda, was "N-E-N," which was theological shorthand for "No Explanation Necessary."

Precious was not an angel; she was not a saint; she was not even dead; yet she was already demanding explanation of Divine Mystery. Indeed, why bother dead at all if you could get such clarification during your lifetime? When she was good and dead the Master Plan would be duly clarified, the mystery and role of the out of order dog solved. Until such time it was her duty to tidy up her corner of the world and hush up with the questions before Massah God got fed up with the nagging and flogged her with a pox.

The pastor had similarly glib explanations for everything that had befallen her. For example, it was quite clear to him that Jamaican Jesus had really been Satan in disguise and that all along Precious had been crawling under her bed to hold chummy chat with Lucifer. He inferred the true identity of Jamaican Jesus from Precious's account that the imposter often used raw patois. According to Precious, this bogus Jesus would sometimes greet her under the bed with the patois, "A wa a gwan, Precious?" meaning, "What's going on, Precious?" But everyone knew that only ignorant ole negar and uncouth Lucifer talked patois and that Jesus would sooner climb up back on the cross than garble, "A wa a gwan." Moreover, real Jesus was not a bed bug; He did not rendezvous with His congregation under a filthy mattress.

"My mattress is not filthy!" Precious shot back angrily. "I air it out and beat it at least three times a year!"

But really, Precious had no good argument to refute the pastor's theories. She was not at all convinced that "N-E-N" was the right answer and suspected that she was being bullyridden with argument on her own front porch. Nor could she explain why Jamaican Jesus had vanished or why she felt certain He would never come back. But because she could think of no clever rejoinder, she could only fidget and listen dumbly.

As the months passed the pastor became such a regular visitor that it was only natural that he should also unburden himself on Precious. One night, for example, he wearily confessed to her that he possessed a hood improperly colossal for a man of the cloth; so grossly endowed was he—this handiwork of Satan daily weighting down his drawers—that his dead wife had screamed and locked herself in the closet the first time she saw him naked.

Precious jumped at once to her feet and ordered him off her veranda. The pastor scolded her for treating a fellow pilgrim's cross with un-Christian harshness, but Precious was unyielding. She was not smart, she declared, but she knew vulgar boasting when she heard it. She ran him off the porch and went to her bed, fuming.

But they made up a few days later after the pastor apologized, saying that he misspoke because of depression over his burdensome cross. Precious did not know whether to box his face or pat him on the back, but because the apology was whispered after services as worshippers in their Sunday best trickled around them in a stream of bobbing heads and murmured greetings, she acknowledged his contrition with a grim nod and a murmur to the effect that, "We are all gunmen, criminals, and sinners."

The pastor said, "Amen, sister," and soon afterwards resumed his regular nighttime visits.

The new Precious slept fearlessly well in her lonely mountain house. When she laid her head down at night it was in a pool of thin mountain air scented with nighttime fragrances and burbling with the background chirrups of insects. Cool breezes soothed her slumbers, and though she occasionally started awake in the deep night with a fluttering heart, she would merely roll over in the bed and mutter philosophically, "Lord, drop de tin can if it please you." In the morning she sometimes added yet another dollop of resignation to the Divine Will, "Bring on de nasty dog, too, if dat is you pleasure."

She took driving lessons, got her license, and bought a secondhand car. She got back her old job at the hotel and had plenty to occupy her weekdays.

An unfulfilled emptiness haunted her weekends, however, especially on Saturday nights. But with the pastor cautiously circling, she had vague prospects of betterment to come. Lately he had begun to passionately kiss her goodnight, and as the weeks passed both the night visits and kisses grew deeper and longer.

Maud still shuffled every day around the lonely house, casting a wary eye on Red Dog and muttering dourly about domestic slavery on a steep and lonely mountaintop. For her part, Precious had come to love the fresh and cooling airs enough to tolerate the loneliness, the clutter of peaks. Indeed, if she must be murdered, she would prefer murder in a cool and breezy place rather than in an airless lowland. And if she must be tied up and raped, she preferred that it be done on her own bed.

Migration to America and the nasty experience with the American dog had taught Precious a lifelong lesson: She now understood that the head of every pilgrim on this earth lay bare and defenseless against the tin can; that neither grooming nor Christian piety was enough to fend off the perverse dog of fate out to wee-wee all over an innocent earthling's foot. In life no woman had final say over outcome or effect. She could choose to wear a certain hat or to walk bareheaded, but it made no difference to heaven's tin can. Whether her foot was naked or shod in leather pumps did not count with heaven's capricious dog. That being the indisciplined nature of this unruly earth, one might as well take to the road bravely without undue fretting.

This was the philosophy of the new Precious.

Chapter 25

Several months after her return, Precious received notice from the village post office of the arrival of a package addressed to her. She immediately drove into the village to get it.

"What a big box you get!" the postmistress announced to Precious over the counter of the dingy shop that also served as a makeshift post office. "Beg you a little help wid it."

Precious walked around the grimy counter and into the smelly back room of the shop, where she helped the postmistress wrestle a cumbersome box through the small side door and into the trunk of her parked car.

She drove home and bellowed for Maud to help. Together, the two of them struggled with the box over the rocky lawn and onto the front veranda.

"Go get a knife for me, Maud," Precious ordered.

Maud returned with the knife and stood peering curiously while Precious carefully cut open the box.

"What could come in such a big box?" the maid wondered aloud, glad for the respite from humdrum cleaning and scrubbing.

"We soon find out now," replied Precious, slitting through the remaining tape.

Craning to stare into the box as Precious opened it, Maud suddenly emitted a piercing squeal of astonishment and jumped backwards.

"Lawd Jesus, mum!" she cried. "Somebody mail you a dog!"

Inside the box, wedged snugly between clumps of styrofoam worms and crumpled newspaper, his snout pasted with the impudent expression he always wore when he squirted Mannish's pants or played woodpecker with Precious's shinbone, crouched freeze-dried Riccardo.

Maud retreated another several feet until she was poised at the edge of the drawing room, ready to bolt into the sanctuary of the kitchen.

"Him dead, mum?" she asked timorously.

"Of course he's dead!" Precious said irritably. "Dey freeze-dried him in America."

"Freeze-dried? Dey can freeze-dry a dog?"

"You don't have any work to do?" snapped Precious, exasperated, reaching into the box and lifting out the dead dog, which was surprisingly light. From the bottom of the box she retrieved a hand-addressed envelope.

"Lawd Jesus," Maud moaned, withdrawing into the order and sanity of her kitchen, "dey freeze-dry dog in America! I must see dat place wid me own eye before I dead."

Steeling herself for bad news, Precious nervously tore open the envelope.

Inside was a note written in a neat hand on personalized stationery with the letterhead inscription: *From the kitchen of Mannish Chaudhuri.* It said:

Dear Precious,

I am taking the liberty to post you Riccardo from Montego Bay where Beulah and I enjoyed a delayed honeymoon and to which I carried him in my suitcase, to spare you difficulties with Customs. (My cousin is right: A freeze-dried dog is very portable.) Beulah says that dog fur makes her sneeze. Plus, she thinks this dog particularly ugly. Rather than throwing him away, I thought it only right that you should have him.

Your troubles with the mistress are past. She has completely accepted my explanations for the dog's disappearance. You were too hasty to leave, for you are utterly forgiven.

Love,
Mannish

p.s. Good news! I have been with Beulah only seven months, but already I have repaid one camel.

There was a noisy row that night between Precious and her pastor, who objected to the display of a freeze-dried rival in the respectable drawing room of the woman he was courting. Precious tartly reminded him that it was her drawing room, that no collection had been taken up in church to pay her mortgage, and grumbling bitterly the pastor walked over to where the lifeless dog crouched in a solitary diorama, turned it over, and blared out an accusing "Aha!" as he pointed an indignant finger at a quarter-inch extrusion of raw dog hood. Precious blinked and heard the cousin's mocking laugh.

"De only rightful thing to do with this dog," the pastor declared huffily, "is to make him a burnt offering. We can build a funeral pyre in de backyard and fire up de dog with a prayer. Like Abraham wid him lamb."

"I don't want to do dat."

"Why not? Why you want dis stinking dog in a respectable drawing room?"

"I just don't feel to do dat."

"Why?" thundered the pastor.

Precious stumbled about trying to think of a reason, but she could utter none to appease him. He pressed his case for making the dog a burnt offering. They were in courtship, and he was a man of the cloth who knew what vile liberty the dog had attempted to take with his future wife. As a Jamaican national, not to mention an ordained minister, he was deeply offended that his wife-to-be would wish to retain a replica of a rapist American dog in her drawing room, the scene of his own warmhearted wooing. Precious stuck to her guns. They had a furious quarrel that ended with the pastor stomping out of the house and roaring off into the night.

The pastor stayed away for three nights. On the fourth he returned complaining of her heartlessness. He sat on the veranda and begged her at least to please shift the dog effigy to a spot where he did not have to endure the animal's faultfinding stare. Precious tucked the dog behind a stuffed chair.

Clearing his throat as if he was about to deliver a eulogy at the funeral of a known crook, the pastor renewed his courtship.

A few evenings later, they were basking contentedly on the veranda in a cool breeze with the pastor trying to persuade Precious to feel up the gabardine hillock over which his zipper zigzagged when they heard a car rattle deep in the throat of the long driveway and saw splinted headlight beams stab the night sky.

Soon the throb of an engine and the squeals of springs grew louder and a car roared up the final gradient and spurted onto the level apron of lawn.

They sat still on the porch and stared while the dogs hurtled from under the house and eddied around the car with a fierce barking. Precious turned on the outside lights, peered into the glare, and heard a familiar voice cry, "Precious, it's Lucy Johnston!"

"Lawd Jesus," Precious gasped, digging her nails into the arm of her pastor. "Is Mistress Lucy!"

"Is your soul cleansed? Have you fear of secret sin?" the pastor scoffed. "Buck up and trust in de Lord, Precious."

"My soul is cleansed," she hissed spitefully, "only because I didn't heed your call to do nasty feeling-up."

She walked boldly down the veranda stairs and over the bumpy lawn to peer cautiously into the darkened car where Mistress Lucy looked back at her from the passenger seat. Beside her sat a muscular stone-faced white man whose eyes darted coldly over the snarling dogs.

Precious timorously greeted her former mistress, shooed the dogs, and the two women pecked at each other with small talk as they settled uncomfortably on the veranda. The man remained in the car, boring his gaze into the dark cellar where the dogs had been driven.

In the watery yellow of the veranda light Precious got her first good look at her former mistress and gasped. She looked as if she were being hollowed-out, devoured from inside by a slow-gnawing worm. Over her gaunt features curdled a deathbed shallowness.

"I'm sick," the mistress quipped in response to Precious's gaping. "But it's six hundred and fifty million American dollars against one disease. Who do you think'll win?"

The pastor drew a sharp, audible breath at this stupendous number. Precious felt weary and heavy-hearted, for she could plainly see who was winning.

"Precious, can we talk alone?" the mistress asked, glancing impatiently at the hovering pastor.

"I beg your pardon, ma'am," the pastor said, standing up and touching his brow in a ludicrously formal salute. "I'm Pastor Wilburn Clarke. How do you do? I will now leave you good ladies to hold solitary converse."

Then he rumbled away into the kitchen. Mistress Lucy stared suspiciously after him before she turned to Precious.

"You didn't have to run away, Precious. Mannish explained everything. I would have understood. I felt I had to see you to tell you that." She gestured at the dark figure hulking in the car. "It cost me nearly $15,000 to track you down. Private detectives like him aren't cheap."

Precious waved her hand helplessly and mumbled, groping to fathom Mannish's possible explanation.

"You didn't mean to hurt Riccardo. Men die between the legs of women every day. And so does the occasional dog."

"Mistress Lucy!" Precious cried, reeling in her chair.

"Don't you see, Precious?" the mistress said intensely, her sickly face lusterless and bruised like the dark side of the moon. "The same thing happened to Barbarosa. I would have understood. I would have grieved with you. We could have mourned together. You didn't have to run away!"

Precious sprang to her feet, protestations churning angrily inside her. She inhaled mountain air and felt the giddy intoxication of nighttime scents and righteousness. She raised her hand to point, perhaps to smite, and glared at the mistress, who slumped in the chair and looked up at her with a feeble crinkle of sickly, querulous wonder.

But Precious did not bellow, and she did not smite, and she did not explode. She had expanded and gained ominous mass that could have detonated at any moment, but she deflated with a resigned wheeze, stalked into the drawing room, and returned carrying the effigy of Riccardo by the scruff of its neck.

Her eyes brimming with tears, the mistress settled the petrified dog upright in her lap like a cannon, its snout aiming a muzzleful of white teeth at the gingerbread rinding the veranda.

"We women carry such frightening power between our legs, Precious," Mistress Lucy whispered with a shudder.

Chapter 26

There was an awful, raging argument on the quiet veranda after the mistress had driven away and the last rattle of her car slapped harmlessly against the dark and bony mountains. The pastor raised his voice so loud and thundered such fury that cows began to low deep in the distant pastures. Precious should not have said that she had slept with the dog unless she really had slept with the dog, and she had sworn to him that she had not slept with the dog. How could he woo a woman who had just confessed that she had killed a dog with her pum-pum? Precious should have boxed the face of that nasty American woman and ordered her off her porch. She should have flung the freeze-dried dog in her face to carry back to America.

Precious sat still and stony and raised her head occasionally to ask what business did he have to eavesdrop on her personal conversation? and who told him to listen? and please not to raise his voice and make her ears ring in the lateness of the night for she had to work tomorrow.

The pastor was beside himself with vexation. He stomped over to her chair, thrust his face provokingly near her nose, seared her with a fiery glare, and bellowed, "Did you or did you not grind de dog?"

Precious got up with disdain and moved out of range of ministerial exhale.

"I did not," she said with dignity.

"But you tell dat woman dat my future wife not only grind her dog, but grind him to death! Now I can never migrate to America!"

He said more. He bellowed up and down the chromatic scale of fit and fury. And when he was spent and wasted and reduced to a quivering mass of impotent rage, Precious got up and calmly announced that she was retiring to bed.

"Precious, just answer me one question," he begged from the top of the veranda stairs as she prepared to latch the door. "Why in heaven's name did you tell dat woman dat you grind de dog to death if you didn't even grind de dog?"

Precious squinted hard and long at him. She shrugged and said, "N-E-N."

Then she went defiantly, unrepentantly, to her empty bed.

Also from **AKASHIC BOOKS**

THE LUNATIC by Anthony C. Winkler
244 pages, trade paperback, $14.95

"The author never relaxes his hilarious examination of the island's taboos . . . By far the funniest book I've read in a decade, although its ribald atmosphere is sprayed with the pepper-gas of aggressive social satire."
—*Washington Post Book World*

THE GIRL WITH THE GOLDEN SHOES
By Colin Channer, afterword by Russell Banks
172 pages, trade paperback original, $13.95

"*The Girl with the Golden Shoes* is a nearly perfect moral fable."
—Russell Banks, author of *Continental Drift*

"[M]oving, beautifully constructed, and morally complex."
—Chris Abani, author of *The Virgin of Flames*

SHE'S GONE by Kwame Dawes
340 pages, trade paperback original, $15.95

"Dawes offers vibrant characters and locales in this diaspora of black culture and strong emotions, bordering the fine line between love and madness between two troubled people."
—*Booklist*